"What was Ginger saying?" Joshua asked.

"She said not to let you monopolize all my time."

He sighed. "And what did you say to that? Because I was… I was kind of hoping you'd let me walk around and introduce you."

Phoebe pressed her lips together, not sure how to respond.

She met his gaze. "Do you have a girl?"

He shook his head.

She felt her heart give a little trip. "Sweet on someone?"

He tilted his head. "You could say that."

Against her will, Phoebe felt an overwhelming sense of disappointment. She looked down at the grass at her feet. "Then you should go be with her."

He was quiet so long that at last she looked up at him and found him studying her.

"I can't," he said very quietly.

She held his gaze, feeling a little light-headed. She remembered this fee_____ __ ___ felt it in those early days and months v_____ _____ courted. She nibbled on _____ _____ she dared.

He hesitated, then shru___ _____ with her."

Emma Miller lives quietly in her old farmhouse in rural Delaware. Fortunate enough to have been born into a family of strong faith, she grew up on a dairy farm, surrounded by loving parents, siblings, grandparents, aunts, uncles and cousins. Emma was educated in local schools and once taught in an Amish schoolhouse. When she's not caring for her large family, reading and writing are her favorite pastimes.

Books by Emma Miller

Love Inspired

The Amish Spinster's Courtship
The Christmas Courtship

The Amish Matchmaker

A Match for Addy
A Husband for Mari
A Beau for Katie
A Love for Leah
A Groom for Ruby
A Man for Honor

Hannah's Daughters

Courting Ruth
Miriam's Heart
Anna's Gift
Leah's Choice

Visit the Author Profile page at Harlequin.com for more titles.

The Christmas Courtship

Emma Miller

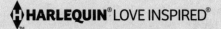
HARLEQUIN® LOVE INSPIRED®

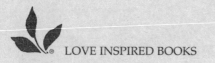

LOVE INSPIRED BOOKS

Recycling programs
for this product may
not exist in your area.

ISBN-13: 978-1-335-47949-5

The Christmas Courtship

For if ye forgive men their trespasses, your heavenly Father will also forgive you.
—*Matthew* 6:14

Chapter One

Dover, Delaware

At the convenience store that served as the Greyhound bus station, Joshua held open the door for an Englisher. Dressed in a puffy white coat, the elderly woman stared up at him, her mouth agape, as she walked through the doorway. Maybe she wasn't used to seeing an Amish man in a 7-Eleven, or maybe it was his Ray-Ban sunglasses that surprised her. He offered a half smile and removed them as he walked into the store.

He was looking for his stepmother's cousin.

He'd seen the bus pull out as he'd secured his horse and buggy to a lighting pole in the parking lot. She had to be here. He scanned the aisles. He spotted a woman and a little boy getting milk from one of the cold cases, and a tall, slender man considering his candy selection. Just Englishers.

He exhaled impatiently. A trip to the bus station hadn't been on his list of things to do that day. He'd had previous plans. He and his stepsister were supposed to get together this afternoon to talk about their idea of opening a greenhouse and garden shop the following spring. He'd been eager to finally sit down with Bay Laurel and get their ideas on paper. Instead, he was running errands for his stepmother, Rosemary.

Rosemary had married his widower father two years ago, and Joshua couldn't have been happier. Joshua adored Rosemary and he'd do anything for her. Which was why he was at the bus station on a cold, blustery November day looking for a cousin who was supposed to be here. He didn't even know what Phoebe looked like. He'd never met her. But how hard could it be to find an Amish woman in a 7-Eleven?

"Need something?" asked an enormous man from behind the checkout counter. He had a beard as long and bushy as any Amish elder's.

Joshua glanced at the Englisher. "Looking for a girl."

The man laughed from deep in his belly. "Aren't we all."

Joshua didn't laugh. He didn't even smile. He wasn't offended; he just didn't get Englisher humor sometimes. "An Amish girl. She should have gotten off the bus." He pointed in the direction of the parking lot.

"Haven't seen her."

Joshua hooked his thumbs into his denim pants pockets and sighed with exasperation. He wasn't sure what to do. He had no idea how to find out if Rosemary's cousin had actually been on the bus or not. For all he knew, she could have changed her mind and never boarded in Pennsylvania. Apparently, her parents were sending Phoebe to Kent County because she'd been involved in some sort of scandal. Word was she'd have a better chance of finding a husband outside her hometown. Of course, among the Old Order Amish, asking for someone's secret apple streusel recipe could be considered a scandal, so the idea that the poor girl was coming to them in disgrace didn't hold much water with him.

Joshua stared at a display of potato chips in front of him, wondering if he should give his stepmother a call. They didn't have a phone in their house. The Amish didn't have telephones. It was one of the ways they held themselves apart from others. But his family *did* have a phone in his father's harness shop. Most bishops allowed their congregants to have phones for their businesses as long as it wasn't inside the home. Sadly, more and more Amish needed cell phones for work purposes because more Amish men were forced to work in the Englisher world for financial reasons. But those phones were never left on or carried in pants pockets. They were stowed in pantry drawers and more creative places. One of his neighbors stored his in his chicken house.

Joshua saw no point in calling the harness shop and relaying a message to Rosemary in the house because if the cousin had decided not to come, how would Rosemary know? From what his stepmother had said, Phoebe came from an extremely conservative Amish community in Pennsylvania. She certainly didn't have a telephone.

Joshua glanced at the man at the cash register again.

He was wearing a camouflage T-shirt and pants, and a bright orange knit cap advertising some kind of sports drink. Despite the clothes, he didn't look like much of a hunter.

"You sure you haven't seen an Amish girl?" Joshua asked. "She would have come inside. It's too cold to wait out there. Probably wearing a black bonnet and long black cloak," he said, trying to jog the man's memory.

The guy placed his meaty hands on the counter and leaned forward. "Look, buddy, I haven't seen any gal in prairie wear today. I know what your people look like. They come in once in a while."

Debating what to do, Joshua watched the customer who'd been looking over the candy approach the register. He'd gone with the chocolate peanut butter cups. Joshua liked those, too.

A door opened in the back of the store and a woman's voice caught his attention.

"*Atch*, you're so welcome." She had a Pennsylvania *Deutsch* lilt to her words. The language, which was equivalent to High German, was what his people spoke.

Joshua turned to see an Amish woman in a black bonnet and black floor-length wool cloak holding a baby bundled in a blanket. There was an Englisher woman with her who was wearing, over her head, a brightly colored scarf that covered her hair.

"I hope your father is here soon," the Amish woman said to the other woman. Then she raised the little one in her arms and peered into his face. The baby looked to be about five or six months old. "Nice to meet you, Amir. Be a good boy for your mama." She passed the baby to the Englisher.

"Phoebe?" Joshua called across the store. "Phoebe Miller?"

"*Ya?*" The Amish woman turned to him, seeming as surprised by Joshua as he was of her.

He'd had a picture in his mind of what Rosemary's cousin would look like: a meek mouse of a girl, small, plump and plain, with dishwater-brown hair and maybe wire-frame spectacles. He supposed what Rosemary had said about her being sent away by her parents had brought him to those conclusions. But this Phoebe was neither plump nor plain. And she was no mouse of a girl. She was tall, almost as tall as he was, and pretty, with corn silk blond hair and startling blue eyes.

"Where were you?" he asked, walking toward her. His tone came out as curt, more because he was taken off guard by her appearance than because he was annoyed that he hadn't been able to find her. "I've been looking for you."

Phoebe turned to the young woman with the child and said something he couldn't hear. The Englisher woman walked away, taking a different aisle toward the front of the store.

"Do you have a suitcase?" Joshua asked Phoebe. Now that he had found her, he was eager to get home. They had to stop at Byler's on the way out of town to pick up some groceries for his stepmother. If he hurried, he might still have time to talk with Bay before it was time to feed up for the evening.

Phoebe picked up a large canvas duffel bag off the floor and walked toward him. "Who are you?"

"Joshua Miller." He put out his hand to take her bag, but she pulled it out of his reach. "Rosemary Miller's son."

She narrowed her eyes, blue eyes with thick, dark lashes. "Her son is a little boy. Jesse," she said suspiciously. "And then she has the babes," she added.

He rolled his eyes, adjusting his wide-brimmed black hat to get a better look at her. That she was awfully pretty being his first conclusion. And spirited was his second. Again, not what he was expecting. It wasn't his experience that Amish women her age questioned Amish men they didn't know. "I'm Rosemary's *stepson*. She married my father, Benjamin, two years ago. She would have come herself, but she just had surgery on her foot and she's supposed to stay off it. My little brothers born to Rosemary are Josiah and James. Believe me now?"

"Maybe," she retorted.

There was something about her tone of voice that nearly made him chuckle. "Anything else you'd like to quiz me on?" he asked, raising an eyebrow.

"You're Benjamin's son, you say?"

"You know him?" He slid on his sunglasses, wishing he'd put on his good coat instead of the one he usually wore to the barn. This one had a tear on the sleeve. He hoped it didn't smell like cow dung. He'd milked this morning with his twin brother, Jacob. There was something about the way she looked at him that made him want to impress her. Or at least not give a bad first impression.

"I don't know Benjamin, but my mother knew who he was when Rosemary wrote to us to tell us she was remarrying." Phoebe stood there in the convenience store aisle still gripping her bag, now with both hands.

"Are we related?" he asked. "You know, having the same name." The moment the words came out of his mouth, he regretted them. Of course, she knew what he meant. He'd just introduced himself as Joshua Miller, and she knew who his father was. Of course, she knew they shared the same surname.

"*Ne*, we're not related, just the same last name. Lots of Amish Millers."

He nodded, strangely relieved that they weren't related by blood. "We've got Millers in Hickory Grove we're not related to. People are always getting my father confused with Al Miller," he explained. He watched the woman with the baby walk down the aisle next to them. "You know her?" he asked quietly, nodding in the Englisher woman's direction.

Phoebe glanced in the stranger's direction, smiled and then looked back at him. "Met her on the bus. Her name is Daneen. She's from New Jersey, come to Delaware to see her parents. I was just holding the baby for her while she washed her hands."

It occurred to Joshua that some Amish girls might be uncomfortable helping out, or even speaking to someone who looked so different from them. Most Amish women had very little contact with Englishers...of any sort. He was impressed. And intrigued. And feeling a little out of sorts now because she seemed very worldly to him. Not in a bad way, just more experienced in life. And he was pretty certain she was older than he was.

He cleared his throat. "So, um...you think it's safe to ride to Hickory Grove with me?" he asked. "Now that you know Rosemary must really have sent me." He put his hand out for her bag again.

"I suppose so. But I can carry it myself." She walked past him, headed for the door.

"See you found your girl," the guy in the camo called

to Joshua as he followed Phoebe past the checkout register.

Joshua put his head down and didn't answer, but the thought went through his head... *Maybe I have.*

Phoebe stood behind the grocery cart watching Joshua place multiple boxes of cereal in the basket.

"I know this looks like a lot, but my brothers and I, we can eat." He flashed her a grin as he put two more boxes into the cart. He was up to eight: three boxes of bran flakes with raisins, three boxes of wheat biscuits and two boxes of something with marshmallows. He'd said that his little stepbrother, Jesse, loved marshmallows. "My *dat* has five boys and one daughter. My sister's married. She and her husband decided to stay in New York when we moved here two years ago. My twin, Jacob, and I are the youngest. All five of us boys live at home. Then there's Rosemary's children. Even with my stepsister Lovey married and living down the road, there are the four girls, then Jesse and the babies." He tugged at the cart and she gave a push. "That means twelve of us at every meal, plus the two littles, and that's if Lovey and her husband, Marshall, don't come by, which they do all the time." He chuckled. "We had to build a second kitchen table so we could all sit down to eat at the same time."

Phoebe smiled to herself as he went on. Even though she knew she'd done the right thing in leaving Pennsylvania, she'd still been nervous about coming to Rosemary's and meeting her extended family. She hadn't seen her cousin in years, and then to come under these circumstances, it was more than a little overwhelming. And then when it wasn't Rosemary who came to pick her up, but her son. Her stepson. That had really set Phoebe off-kilter. At the bus stop, Joshua had seemed annoyed with her, at least at first, because he couldn't find her. But it had been the right thing to do, to hold Amir for Daneen while she used the ladies' room. Phoebe knew what it was like to try to do day-to-day tasks with a baby in your arms all the time and no one to help you. And she'd only been in the ladies' room for a few minutes.

Phoebe glanced at Joshua again. She had liked him at once. Despite his irritation with her back at the bus stop, he seemed to be good-natured.

He pulled the grocery cart forward and began to put bags of rolled oats into it. She'd never seen an Amish man grocery shop by himself before. Her stepfather had never stepped foot in a grocery store, let alone shopped on his own.

"...a lot of confusion the first few weeks after we arrived from New York, the twelve of us," Joshua was saying. "Lovage didn't come with us, straight off. She stayed to see her mother's farm sold." He'd been talking since they left the bus station. Which was fine with Phoebe because then she didn't have to talk. Not talking meant not having to answer questions.

"But then we found our footing." Joshua added some granola bars to the cart. "Hickory Grove is a nice place. I think you'll like it. We do."

She smiled at him as he went on. He was nice-looking, Rosemary's stepson. Joshua was around Phoebe's own age, maybe a little younger. He had reddish-brown hair that curled at the back of his neck beneath his black knit hat and a handsome face, with dark eyes and a strong brow. His face was clean-shaven, which meant he was unmarried. Which of course made sense since he still lived at home. She had known the man Rosemary had wed had children from his previous marriage, but she hadn't known he had adult sons.

"*Ne?* Never been?" Joshua asked.

Phoebe looked up, realizing he had asked her a question. She shook her head. "I'm sorry. What did you say?"

He gripped the end of the cart so they were looking at each other, her on one side, him on the other. He had nice hands: strong, with squared-off nails that were clean. "It's all right," he told her. "I talk too much."

"It's not that at all," she said.

"*Ne,* I talk too much. Everyone in my family says so. I talk when I'm nervous and when I'm not. I talk when I'm happy and when I'm sad. When I was little my mother used to say that she put me to bed talking and I picked right up on the sentence come dawn the next day."

Phoebe struggled to hide a smile. His cheerfulness lightened her heart. He made her hopeful that this move had been the right thing for her to do. "I'm enjoying hearing about your family," she said. "It sounds like you all get along so well. Your father's children and Rosemary's. It can't be easy making two families into one. It's not as if you're little ones."

"It's not always easy. Mornings when we have to get out of the house for church can be tense." He shrugged. "But we're working on it. Once a week we sit down together and eat a bunch of desserts and talk about whatever's bugging us." He shrugged. "Whether it's my brother Jacob not taking his turn cleaning horse stalls or our stepsister Ginger hogging the upstairs bathroom."

He turned down the baking aisle, still pulling the cart along. Phoebe followed.

"But my father and Rosemary are so happy together," he told her over his broad shoulder. "They love each other. So we're all determined to make it work. *All of us*," he said with conviction.

Phoebe smiled at him again, this time making no attempt to hide it.

He knitted his brows. "What?"

She felt her cheeks grow warm. She was tempted not to tell him why she was smiling, but it wasn't really in her nature not to answer an honest question with an honest answer. "You said your father and Rosemary love each other. I don't think I've ever heard a man say such a thing."

"Say what thing?"

"Speak of love," she responded quietly. "It's not very Amish, is it?"

He thought for a moment. "My father's a man who doesn't hide how he feels and he doesn't mind telling you, good or bad. I guess I take after him."

Phoebe looked up to see an Amish girl of about twenty with a woman who was likely her mother approaching them. They were each pushing a grocery cart overflowing with boxes of cereal, flour and sugar, and bags and bags of cookies, snack cakes and potato chips.

The younger of the two women caught sight of Joshua, giggled and looked away.

"Joshua?" The older woman acknowledged him and

stopped her cart, blocking other customers, Amish, English and Mennonite, from continuing down the aisle. She was a small, round woman with rectangular wire-frame glasses who fluttered her hands, reminding Phoebe a little bit of a bumblebee. "How's Rosemary doing with the foot? Staying off it, I hope?" She was speaking to Joshua, but she was staring Phoebe down.

"Doing well, Eunice. Had an appointment yesterday with the doctor." He reached for a ten-pound bag of whole wheat flour. He didn't seem to notice that Eunice was gawking at Phoebe. "Doctor says surgery went well. Healing fine. Back on her feet in no time, as good as ever."

Phoebe watched him add another bag of whole wheat flour to the cart. She didn't recall flour being on the grocery list he'd shared with her on the way from the bus station to the store.

"Who does she see? Dr. Gallagher, is it, or Dr. Parker?"

Joshua shook his head. "I wouldn't know." He added yet another ten-pound bag of flour to the cart.

"It's no wonder she needed that surgery." Eunice glanced at Joshua and then returned her attention to Phoebe.

The young woman was staring at a box of cereal but stealing glances at Joshua. She obviously found him attractive.

Phoebe was beginning to feel uncomfortable now. It wasn't that she wasn't used to people staring at her. She was even used to whispers behind her back. But she hadn't expected this here. Or at least she had hoped it wouldn't happen. And at once she wondered how much

Eunice knew about her and her *circumstances*, as her mother liked to put it.

"Chasing after two toddlers at *her* age." Eunice made a clicking sound of disapproval between her teeth. "How old will she be come next year?"

Joshua smiled sweetly at Eunice. "I don't know. You'd have to ask Rosemary." He leaned around Eunice. "Good to see you, Martha. Visiting your aunt again, are you?"

Martha giggled and pushed her glasses up farther on her nose. *"Ya."*

"What are you doing here at Byler's?" Eunice asked. "None of your stepsisters could make it today?"

"They could." Joshua added a huge bag of chocolate chips to the cart.

Also not on the list, Phoebe noted.

"But I like grocery shopping," Joshua said.

Eunice drew back with a harrumph.

Joshua leaned around Eunice again to speak to Martha. "Rosemary's cousin is visiting, too," he told the younger woman. "This is Phoebe."

Martha gave a quick nod, giggled and gave her glasses another push at the bridge of her nose.

Phoebe glanced behind Martha. There was a long line of customers behind her in the aisle now, waiting to get by or move forward.

"Visiting, are you?" Eunice said to Phoebe, her face lighting up with interest. "From where? Rosemary didn't say she had a cousin visiting. I was just there two days ago at her sickbed. She never mentioned a word."

"We need to go, Eunice," Joshua said, intervening in the conversation. "Have to get these things home and we're holding other folks up." He nodded in the direction of the customers lined up behind Eunice and Martha and their grocery carts. Then, for good measure, he reached out and gave Eunice's cart a little push.

Phoebe didn't know why, but that struck her as funny, and she had to look away so Eunice wouldn't catch her smiling.

"I suppose you're right," Eunice huffed with obvious disappointment. She grabbed the handle of the cart with both hands and gave it a shove. "Tell Rosemary I said hello and for her to stay off that foot. Tell her I'll be by at the end of the week."

"Will do," Joshua said as Eunice passed them, discernibly reluctant to move on. When Martha passed, he nodded to her.

The minute they were gone, Joshua leaned on the end of his cart, drawing closer to Phoebe. "Sorry about that," he murmured, meeting her gaze.

She placed her hands on the handle and leaned forward, her words meant only for him. "Town gossip?"

"Editor of the Amish telegraph." Joshua's eyes twinkled.

He had nice eyes, brown with thick lashes. Expressive eyes.

"No news she doesn't know and readily share," he told her. "True or otherwise."

Phoebe couldn't help herself. She laughed and then felt self-conscious. People were pushing past them with their shopping carts, some looking with interest at her and Joshua leaning across the cart whispering to each other.

"How'd you know?" he asked.

"Ours is Lettice Litwiller. I think they look alike," she teased. "She and Eunice."

He laughed and slapped his hand on the edge of the cart. Then he grabbed a bag of flour from the cart and lifted it out with ease.

"What are you doing?" Phoebe asked, watching him return the bag to the shelf.

"Putting it back. We don't need flour." He reached for another bag.

Phoebe picked up the third and pushed it onto the shelf. "Why did you put it in the cart, then?"

He shrugged. "I don't know." He returned the bag of chocolate chips, too. "Just because I know it annoys Eunice to no end that Rosemary has no problem getting us boys to sweep a porch or pick up some milk on the way home from town and she can't get her own sons to pick up their dirty clothes from the floor." He grabbed the cart and started forward, then halted again. He curled his finger to draw her closer again.

Phoebe knew their behavior bordered on inappropriate. Amish men and women were not generally so friendly with each other and certainly not in public. They didn't laugh and whisper to each other. And a woman like her, a woman who'd nearly been shunned, definitely had no business carrying on with a man this way.

"That," Joshua said, his tone conspiratorial, "and I want to see how long it takes to get around the neighborhood that Rosemary had one of her stepsons buy thirty pounds of whole wheat flour and a huge bag of chocolate chips." He laughed. "Bet she'll have Rosemary baking cookies for the whole county." He raised his eyebrows. "Something new for the Amish telegraph."

Phoebe met Joshua's gaze over the grocery cart and smiled, not just because she liked his silliness, but because she was pretty certain she'd made her first friend in a very long time.

Chapter Two

Her cousin Rosemary's home looked just like Phoebe thought it would. It was a rambling white clapboard farmhouse, two stories with multiple additions, rooflines running in several directions and two red chimneys to anchor the proportions. The land was flat, no hills and valleys like home, but beautiful in its own way even in the dry bareness of autumn. There were barns, sheds and small outbuildings galore, painted red, all dwarfed by the enormous old dairy barn that Joshua explained housed Benjamin's harness shop. There, the family not only made and repaired leather goods like bridles and harnesses, but also sold items like axle grease, horse liniments and other items Amish and English customers were in need of.

"We sell eggs, too," Joshua said as they drove up the crushed oyster shell driveway, past the parking lot, where there were two black buggies tied to a hitching post, an old pickup and a little blue sedan parked. "My sister Bay—" He glanced at Phoebe, the reins in his gloved hands. "I'm just going to tell you now, we dropped the *step* part ages ago. So, when you hear one of us say brother or sister or daughter or son, we might mean that we're not actually related by blood, but we're all family now."

"Got it." She nodded and smiled to herself, happy for them, a little sad for herself. In the home where she'd grown up, her stepfather had never let her forget that she was a stepchild, which had somehow translated to mean she was something less than his own children. Phoebe's father had taken ill when she was just a baby and died. Her mother had remarried a year later and Phoebe had become the stepdaughter of Edom Wickey, an authoritarian, dogmatic man who easily saw all of the ills of the world but never the good.

"So, anyway," Joshua went on, pulling Phoebe back into the conversation. "My sister Bay Laurel, we call her Bay, sells eggs and sometimes frying chickens out of the shop. I think they're adding jams and such. Oh, and she sells our sister Nettie's quilts, too. Only Nettie doesn't just do quilts. She makes these hanging things." He gestured in the air with one gloved hand. "I guess Englishers put them on their walls? Like for—" He seemed to search for the right word in Pennsylvania *Deutsch*, then switched to English. "Decoration?" He clamped the reins with both hands again. "Don't get me wrong. They're beautiful, but I don't get having something that just hangs there and serves no purpose. They can be beautiful on a bed and more useful, right? She does all kinds of patterns—the old ones like Garden of Eden, Jacob's ladder, Joseph's coat. But she's made some of her own patterns, too. She made this one that looked like a nest but was made of tree limbs that—"

He went quiet and lowered his head. "I'm talking too much again."

"You're not. *Ne*, you're not," Phoebe insisted, reaching over and touching his arm. The moment she felt his warmth through the thick denim of his homemade coat, she snatched her hand back and gazed out the side window of the buggy.

Amish men and women didn't whisper and laugh together in grocery stores, and they certainly didn't touch casually. She could almost hear her stepfather's angry scolding ringing in her ears.

Suddenly tears welled in her eyes. Hoping Joshua didn't see them, she blinked them away. She didn't know why she was suddenly so emotional. She was here in Hickory Grove because she wanted to be. She was here because she knew it was the right thing for her. And for John-John.

"Here we are," Joshua announced as he reined in the bay and the buggy rolled to a halt. If he noticed she had touched him, or her response, he didn't show it.

Phoebe glanced up to see two half-grown puppies that were a rich chestnut color bounding down the front porch steps, barking excitedly.

"That would be Silas and Adah. Chesapeake Bay retrievers. My brother Jacob raises and sells them," Joshua explained.

As the dogs ran around the front of the buggy, Phoebe realized each was missing one rear leg. They appeared to have been born that way. She took in her breath sharply, not because she had never seen an animal with a disability, but because it didn't seem to hinder their speed or frivolity one bit.

"*Ya*, only three legs apiece. That's why Jacob couldn't sell them. Or wouldn't." He wrapped the reins around the brake lever, and the bay danced in its traces. "And he couldn't stand the idea of seeing them put down, even though our vet said he wouldn't be unwarranted to do it." He glanced at her. "My brother named them after these neighbors we had in New York. Silas and Adah Snitzer. They were brother and sister. One was blind, the other deaf. They took care of each other. Led a full, good, Godly life."

Phoebe knitted her brow. "You don't think your neighbors would mind having dogs named after them?"

"They passed away a few years ago. Were in their nineties. Died within a day of each other." He smiled, seeming lost in the memory of them. "But I think they would have liked the idea that Jacob named his dogs after them." He chuckled and then slammed his thigh. "Well, guess we best go inside and get you settled. That's my brother Jesse there on the porch. Rosemary's boy." He pointed. "Waiting for us, I suspect."

Phoebe looked over to see a boy of ten or so with neatly trimmed brown hair and a sweet, lopsided smile hurrying across the covered porch toward them.

"I'm warning you now," Joshua said as he opened the buggy door and climbed down. "He'll talk your ear off if you let him." He chuckled. "Not unlike me, I guess."

Phoebe smiled but didn't say anything as she opened her door.

"Want to take Toby up to the barn?" Joshua called to his little brother.

Jesse bounded down the porch steps and across the

driveway, pulling a black wool watch cap down over his head.

On Phoebe's side of the buggy, Joshua offered his hand to help her out of the buggy, but instead of taking it, she handed him her canvas bag. "If you could take this? *Danke*," she said, feeling as if she needed to avoid making physical contact with him.

"Sure." Joshua caught the bag as she practically tossed it down. "Jesse, this is your cousin, Phoebe."

Phoebe climbed down quickly. "Nice to meet you, Jesse." A gust of wind caught the edge of her cloak and whipped it open. Dry brown and gold and orange leaves blew around her. "Goodness." She grasped the edges of the heavy wool and pulled her outer garment tightly around her. "I didn't expect it to be so cold here. I was thinking that because it's farther south…" She let the sentence go unfinished, feeling now like *she* was the one who talked too much.

"Cold snap," Jesse told her. "Nice to have you with us." His words sounded rehearsed, as if his mother had told him what to say when they met. But his smile was genuine.

Jesse turned to his big brother. "I should take Phoebe inside? I can take her bag, too. We're having chicken potpie for dinner." Beaming, he went on faster. "I hope you like chicken potpie. It's my *mam*'s recipe. She puts peas in it. Most people don't, but my *mam* does. Only Mam didn't make it 'cause she's laid up so my sisters made it."

"See what I mean?" Joshua said to Phoebe. He turned to his little brother. "*Ne*, I thought I'd take her in. Can you manage Toby? He needs a good rubdown and a scoop of oats." He handed Phoebe her bag and walked around to the back of the buggy to unload the groceries. "I'll be up directly to help you with her harness."

"I got it," Jesse insisted, grasping the gelding's bridle. Bags in hand, Joshua closed the back of the buggy and his little brother began to lead the horse away, walking backward so he could still see Joshua and Phoebe. "I'll be in shortly. I can show you around if you want, Phoebe. Show you where you'll be sleeping and where the towels are and such."

"Thank you. I'd like that," she called to him as he made his way up the driveway.

"I think he likes you," Joshua said. He led Phoebe up the front steps to the wide porch, the puppies nipping at his heels.

"Some say I have a way with children," she answered absently, glancing at the door that led into the house.

She was suddenly nervous to see her cousin Rosemary again, to meet the rest of the family. They had to all know why she was there. Know what she had done. Her mother had said that Rosemary Stutzman Miller was as nonjudgmental as a soul could be, but it had been years since the cousins had seen each other. What if Rosemary had changed? That sometimes happened as folks aged. They became more rigid in their beliefs and ways. It had been like that with her stepfather. He hadn't softened with age. He'd grown more rigid.

Joshua shifted the sacks of groceries in his arms, opened the door and stepped back. "*Ne!* Get back, you two," he said, laughing as he caught the pups with his booted foot, blocking their entry into the house. He looked up at Phoebe. "Go on in. If I let these two in again today, Rosemary will have me washing dishes for a week. I already accidentally let them in this morning. They made it through the kitchen, down the hall before Jesse caught them."

"Really?" Phoebe asked, unable to hide her surprise. "You and your brothers do *dishes*?" She'd suspected the Miller household was less conservative than her stepfather's, but the Amish stuck to the old ways, and male and female tasks were laid out very explicitly.

"*Ne*, not usually." He laughed again. "We stick mostly to outside chores, but there's no telling what Rosemary will say if I let these two drag mud through her house again."

Phoebe nodded, then walked into the mudroom that looked like so many others she'd passed through. It even looked a lot like her mother's, with rows of denim jackets on hooks, wool cloaks and an assortment of scarves and hats and bonnets on pegboards on the wall. On the floor were piles of boots and shoes in a great array of sizes, some set down neatly, others dropped carelessly. But the moment she stepped into the house, something had immediately felt different about it. Maybe it was her imagination, or maybe it was just the smell of baking apple pie, but Phoebe immediately felt herself relax. Because, somehow, she knew that in this house with its three-legged puppies and chatty little brothers, she would find the acceptance she had never found in her own home.

Talking to the dogs, Joshua closed the door behind Phoebe with his foot. Standing alone in the mudroom, she removed her cloak and black bonnet, found a free hook to hang them on and, travel bag in hand, entered the large but cozy kitchen.

"Goodness, this is hot. Mam, I think we need new pot holders!" a pretty strawberry blonde hollered from the far side of the room, startling Phoebe. Holding an enormous pie in her hands, she tried to close an oven door with her foot.

"I'll get it." Phoebe dropped her bag and hurried to help.

"Thank you," the young woman said, gingerly setting the pie down on a sideboard. She shook her hands, still holding on to the pot holders. "I've been telling Mam for weeks that these were worn-out. Someone is going to get burned one of these days." She grinned. "You must be Phoebe."

Phoebe nodded.

"I'm Tarragon. Call me Tara." She dropped the pot holders on the counter and walked to a massive farmhouse sink. "You're my mother's cousin." She glanced over her shoulder. "Which I guess makes us cousins, too."

Tara smiled again, and Phoebe couldn't help but smile back. Tara was cute as a button, with green eyes and a small, upturned nose. She was wearing a calf-length pink dress and white apron, with a green scarf covering her hair and tied at the back of her neck. Wispy red tendrils peeked out from the scarf around her ears. On her feet, she wore a pair of denim blue sneakers with athletic socks. She looked like a fluttering little songbird in the bright airy kitchen, and Phoebe suddenly felt like an old crow. She was dressed in a black dress, thick black tights and clunky black shoes. She wondered if it was a mistake to think she could ever belong here, make a home here for herself and John-John.

"Ya," Phoebe managed. "Cousins."

"Mam!" Tara hollered, startling Phoebe again. No one ever raised their voice in her house. Words were always spoken softly and soberly.

"Cousin Phoebe's here! Pie's done!" Tara continued loudly. "The blue pot holders are going in the ragbag!"

"She's here?" came a voice from down the hall. "Send her in!"

"Mam just had surgery on her foot. Did Joshua tell you? She's supposed to be keeping it elevated." Tara rolled her eyes. "That's not been easy." She pointed in the direction of the hall. "She's in the parlor. She was so excited when your mother wrote to her about you coming to stay with us."

Phoebe heard the back door open and close, and Joshua's voice. "Jacob's going to have to start kenneling those dogs or teach them to mind people better." He walked into the kitchen carrying the bags of groceries. "See you met Tara," he said to Phoebe.

"Ya, I was just going into the parlor. To see Rosemary."

He set the paper bags down on one of the two enormous kitchen tables in the room. "Let me show you the way."

"It's just down the hall," Tara quipped as she crossed the kitchen to dig into the bags. "You get my cereal? And the butter?"

"Ya, ya, it's all in the bag." Joshua told his stepsister as he motioned to Phoebe. "Come on. Come say hello to Rosemary."

Phoebe followed him down the hall, past a staircase leading to the second floor. At a doorway, he halted. "Here we are," he said to her. "Rosemary, look who I found at the bus station."

Phoebe walked hesitantly to the doorway.

"There you are!"

It was her cousin Rosemary, seated on a sofa, her foot encased in a black cloth boot, propped on a stool. "What took you so long? I was beginning to worry." She opened her arms. "I'd come to you, but this one will have a fit." She pointed to the man seated beside her on the couch. "Benjamin has made me promise I won't get up again until supper."

The burly man with dark hair and a reddish beard rose. Dressed in denim trousers and a long-sleeved blue shirt and suspenders, he wore sheepskin slippers on his short, wide feet. "Now, Rosebud, you know you're not going to heal properly if you don't stay off that foot." He nodded to Phoebe as he walked past her. "*Velcom* to our home. Know our door is open to you and yours always." He met her gaze, something else Phoebe wasn't used to among elder Amish men. "I think this will be a good place for you." He gave her a little smile, his dark brown eyes twinkling. "And will you do me a favor?" he said as he walked past her.

"*Ya...*" His request surprised her. "Of course."

"Keep my wife on that couch until supper. Her foot won't heal if she doesn't rest. There are plenty of able bodies to keep this household going. To care for our little ones." He slipped his thumbs beneath his suspenders. "And now she has you to help as well, *ya*?"

"*Ya...*yes, of course." A little flustered, Phoebe returned her attention to Rosemary as Benjamin left the parlor.

Joshua smiled at Phoebe, lifting his hand in a little wave, and went with his father.

"He worries too much," Rosemary insisted, pointing at her husband as he disappeared down the hall. "Come, Phoebe, give me a hug." She opened her arms wide.

Cousin Rosemary, who had to be in her late forties, could have passed for far younger with her pretty round face and, beneath her white prayer *kapp*, chestnut hair that didn't seem to be graying. Phoebe knew Rosemary had to be nearing menopause because she remembered her mother fussing about Rosemary's advanced age when they'd learned she and her new husband were expecting a baby. Which turned out to be twins. Phoebe hadn't said anything at the time when they'd heard the news because it was always easier to get along with her mother if she agreed with her, but she'd remembered saying a silent prayer when she'd heard the news, thanking God for His goodness in blessing Rosemary and Benjamin.

Phoebe hesitantly crossed the cozy parlor furnished with two couches and two easy chairs covered in flax-colored duck. To her surprise, there were pretty denim blue-and-green square pillows scattered everywhere. There were oak ladder-back chairs along the walls ready to be pulled forward to make more seating, as well as several slightly mismatched oak end tables. In one corner sat a small, round kitchen table and chairs with a stack of game boxes on top. A checkerboard was set up as if just waiting for two players. Like most Amish homes, along one wall there were doors that likely opened into the living room behind it, making a good-sized room for church services. The parlor was very Amish in the way that it was obviously set up for utilitarian use, but it was different in the way that it was so pretty and cozy with its throw pillows and the cross-stitches framed on the walls. And hanging partially over the doors that opened into the living room was an enormous quilt depicting a scene from the Garden of Eden with trees and plants and beautifully plumed birds.

"*Atch*, our Nettie's quilt," Rosemary said, seeing Phoebe staring at it. "Beautiful, isn't it? My daughter has a way with a needle."

"It's *so* beautiful," Phoebe said softly, leaning down to hug Rosemary. She had intended to give her a quick squeeze, but Rosemary wrapped her arms tightly around Phoebe and she wouldn't let her go.

"Everything is going to be okay," Rosemary said quietly in her ear. "Not to worry. God has His plan for you. He has a plan for all of us. We have to be brave enough to be open to it," she whispered.

Tears sprang to Phoebe's eyes. She didn't know if it was her cousin's kind words, full of hope, or just the feeling of another human being's touch that overwhelmed her with emotion. There was no hugging in her stepfather's home. It had been too long since Phoebe had felt someone's arms around her, and suddenly she felt as if she might break down in tears.

"There, there," Rosemary murmured, patting Phoebe's back.

Phoebe sniffed and drew back, pulling a handkerchief from her dress pocket. Embarrassed and not sure what to say, she dabbed at her eyes.

Just then, Tara stuck her head through the doorway. "Apple pie came out nice. I'm going to throw the sweet potato pies in now." She wiped her hands on her apron. "Dough for the rolls is rising already. Anything else you want me to do, Mam?"

Her back to Tara, Phoebe took a moment to dry her eyes and pull herself together.

"Sounds liked you have everything under control, *dochtah*." Rosemary looked up at Phoebe from her perch on the couch. "Wait until you taste Tara's apple pie. You'll be wanting to set a piece aside for breakfast tomorrow. You met, Tara, *ya*?"

"Ya." Phoebe glanced at Tara and nodded.

"I'm Nettie." A slightly older girl came to the doorway, giving a shy wave. She was petite and blond, with her sister's green eyes. In stocking feet, she was wearing a blue dress and a long canvas apron that appeared to be covered with splotches of paint. "The chest of drawers will need just one more coat when I finish this one, and then it will be done, Mam. New knobs and it will be perfect for Phoebe's room." She gave a cautious smile. "I'm sorry I didn't get it done before you arrived. I had two orders for quilts I had to finish before I could start on the chest."

"Nettie found an old chest of drawers at our local farmers market in Dover," Rosemary explained. "Spence's Bazaar is open Tuesdays, Thursdays and Saturdays. We'll take you this week. About anything you want can be bought there—food, produce and all sorts of junk."

"It wasn't junk," Nettie protested, walking over to her mother. She lifted Rosemary's foot in its black boot to readjust the pillow beneath it. Satisfied with the position of her mother's foot, she turned to Phoebe. "I only paid seven dollars for the chest of drawers. Wait until you see it. A couple of repairs, a new coat of paint and the handles I found in our barn, and it's beautiful."

"Nettie likes strays," Tara explained. "Stray cats, stray chests of drawers—"

"You were happy enough with that stray baking pan I bought for you for a dollar last week," Nettie quipped.

Tara wrapped her arms around her waist. "True enough." She glanced at her mother. "Tea, Mam? For you and Phoebe. I managed to hide a couple of ginger-bread cookies from Joshua. He loves gingerbread cook-ies," she explained to Phoebe. "I hardly have the tray out of the oven and he's eaten half a dozen."

"I'm fine until supper," Phoebe said.

"Nonsense." Rosemary shifted her position on the couch. Like her daughters, she was dressed in a calf-length dress, hers blue, and wearing a white prayer bon-net, the ties dangling. "I'm bored. Bring us some of those gingerbread cookies and a pot of mint tea. I gather my own mint and dry it. Makes an excellent tea." She patted the couch indicating Phoebe should approach. "Sit." She glanced up at Nettie as Tara headed for the kitchen. "Join us?"

Nettie eyed the wood-cased clock on the wall. It was handmade, as were the end tables. "Tempting, but— Oh, my, look who's up!" She threw open her arms as another sister Phoebe had not yet met appeared in the doorway. She balanced a sleepy toddler on each hip. "Josiah." Nettie took one of the little boys who was dressed iden-tically to his father in denim trousers and a blue shirt with tiny leather suspenders. "There's my Josiah."

Rosemary put out her arms to take her son from Nettie. "Did you have a nice nap?"

"James was still trying to sleep, weren't you?" the unidentified sister said to the little boy she was still holding. "But big brother Josiah wouldn't let you."

Phoebe saw at once that the little boys who were just over a year old were identical twins.

"You must be Phoebe," the sister said with a smile.

All of Rosemary's daughters were pretty, but this one may have been the prettiest of them all. She was a yellow blonde with the same Stutzman green eyes, but she had a perfect heart-shaped face, thick lashes and rosy cheeks.

"I'm Ginger. And this, in case you didn't know," she said, looking at the little boy in her arms, "is James. Right?" She tickled the little boy, who giggled. "Are you James?"

The sound of the child's laughter struck Phoebe as sharply as if someone had plunged a shard of glass into her chest. "Would he come to me?" she asked, her voice catching in her throat. Suddenly she missed her little boy, her sweet son, so much that she physically felt their separation. She opened her arms to James. Her John-John was only two years older than the twins.

"Want to go to Phoebe?" Ginger asked her little brother. She passed him to Phoebe and the little boy gave no protest.

"There we go," Phoebe murmured, pulling the little boy against her in a hug. He looked up at her with big brown eyes, his father's eyes. "What a good boy," she said softly, shifting him onto her hip.

"Joshua around?" Ginger asked her mother.

"Somewhere," Rosemary responded, offering a little horse to Josiah from a basket of wooden toys beside the couch.

"Need me to watch the boys?" Ginger asked her mother.

"I should finish that coat of paint on the chest of drawers before supper." Nettie tucked a stray lock of hair behind her ear. "But I can stay and watch the boys."

"You can both go about your business," Rosemary insisted. "Phoebe and I can certainly handle two little boys. Can't we?" she asked her son, and he climbed down from her lap, the unpainted toy still clutched in his tiny hand.

"Mam, the doctor was serious about staying off your foot for a couple more days," Nettie warned. "Benjamin said—"

"Benjamin worries more than a *grossmama*." Rosemary plucked another wood toy from behind the cushion on the couch. This one appeared to be a goat. "Phoebe's here. She can give me a hand."

"*Ya,*" Phoebe agreed, fighting tears. She missed her young son immensely, but somehow holding little James gave her comfort.

Spotting the toy in his mother's hand, James wiggled in Phoebe's arms and she reluctantly lowered him to his feet. "They walking yet?" she asked as she set him gently on his feet.

"*Ya*, since they were ten months," Rosemary answered proudly. She waved Ginger and Nettie away. "Shoo. We'll call you if we need you."

Alone with Rosemary and the toddlers, Phoebe lowered herself to the polished, wide-plank wooden floor.

"Would you like that goat, James? What a fine goat," she cooed as he took it from his mother's hand.

For a moment the two women were silent as they watched the boys play. The little ones jabbered to each other, but Phoebe could tell how close they were to speaking their first words. Her John-John had babbled the same way, practicing sounds before finding the words.

"You're missing him?" Rosemary asked softly. "Your son?"

Her tone was so kind that again Phoebe had to struggle to contain her emotion. "Very much."

"How old is he? It's John, isn't it?"

"*Ya*, John. But I call him John-John most of the time." James dropped his toy goat, and Phoebe scooped it up and offered it to him, pretending to make it nibble on his chubby hand before she passed the toy to him. "He's three now," she said. It felt good to talk about him. About her cherished little boy that her family spent most of their time trying to ignore. Trying to pretend he didn't exist.

"A happy child?" Rosemary pressed. "Easygoing?"

"*Ya*, and smart." She looked up at her cousin, her eyes glistened. "And sweet. He's already trying to be helpful. Just yesterday I was folding dishcloths and he wanted to help." She chuckled at the memory. "He made a mess of it of course, but I let him try."

"It's the only way they learn," Rosemary said, chuckling with her.

The women were both silent again for a moment, watching the boys play. Rosemary produced several more hand-carved wooden toys. They were unadorned with paint, but still beautiful and easily recognizable even to a child. There were two chickens, a cow and an animal that took Phoebe a moment to identify.

"Is that…is that a *llama*?" Phoebe asked, watching Josiah try to push the wooden animal beneath the pillow his mother rested her foot on.

"It's an alpaca, a cousin of the llama." Rosemary laughed. "Our vet, Albert Hartman, raises them. Lives over Seven Poplars way. Used to be Mennonite but now he's Amish. Married to my friend Hannah. Anyway, Benjamin took the twins to see them a few weeks ago and our boys were fascinated. I'm just waiting for a trailer to pull up in the barnyard and for Benjamin to unload a herd of alpacas."

Phoebe grinned at the idea.

"Apparently, they can be quite profitable," Rosemary went on. "Or so Benjamin was telling me. I think he was trying to butter me up."

This time, when the women fell into silence again, it was a comfortable one. All of Phoebe's apprehensions about coming to Hickory Grove, her fears that her cousin and family would judge her for her past, were suddenly gone. For the first time in a very long time, she felt at peace. She felt God's nearness and the belief that she was doing what He wanted her to do.

"I want you to know, Phoebe," Rosemary said slowly, "that Benjamin and I think it was very brave of you to come here." She met Phoebe's gaze. "It was the right thing to do for your son."

Phoebe gazed into her cousin's green eyes. "It was kind of you to welcome me." She hesitated. "Considering—"

"Considering what?" Rosemary asked, sounding annoyed with her. "You stumbled. Who of us hasn't?"

Phoebe looked down at her hands folded in her lap. "It was more than a stumble. What I did was a sin."

"Did you love the boy's father?"

Phoebe was surprised by her cousin's forthrightness, but she probably shouldn't have been. Rosemary's family, the environment she raised her family in, was so different than that of her own. *"Ya,"* Phoebe murmured, tears welling in her eyes, against her will. "I loved him, and he loved me. We had made plans to marry, John and I. He—" Her voice caught in her throat. She took a breath and went on. "He had put a deposit down on a farm. We were going to live near a creek," she managed, remembering how happy she had been the day he had taken her in his wagon to see the property. "And then he…he died. A cave-in in his father's silo." She lifted her hands and let them fall into her lap. "And then I had John-John and that was that."

"I understand what our preachers speak of, but don't know that I believe that it's ever a sin to love," Rosemary said thoughtfully.

"Ne," Phoebe argued, taking a toy sheep from the basket and offering it to James. "I sinned. *We* sinned."

"And then you confessed before your bishop and your church," Rosemary countered. "And no more need be said."

Phoebe looked up and saw that Rosemary's eyes were misty. And Phoebe knew in her heart of hearts that everything really was going to be all right.

Chapter Three

Joshua looked up from where he was stacking wood in the wood box as his sister walked into the living room. He was on his knees beside the massive redbrick fireplace. With the cold snap, they'd been burning more wood than they would typically, and he wanted to be sure there was plenty for the evening. With their new guest in the house, he imagined that after supper, when the harness shop was closed and the animals settled for the night, the whole family would retire to the living room. Here, Rosemary and her daughters might knit or do some mending while Joshua, his father and brothers looked over seed catalogs or farm magazines. Tara would probably make popcorn, and they'd sit around together and talk. Someone might tell the family about an exciting or funny or sweet story about a customer at the harness shop. Someone else might relate the antics of one of the animals in the barnyard or news from their community. Occasionally their father would read a story from the Bible or relate a tale from his childhood in the wilds of Canada. It didn't matter what they did or what they talked about—all that mattered was spending an hour or two together as a family. And Joshua wanted Phoebe to be able to experience the comfort of a crackling fire and the sense of wholeness he felt when he sat with his family here in the living room in the evening. Because something told him, something he saw in the depths of her blue eyes, that she didn't have enough of that comfort in her life.

"I've been looking for you." Bay Laurel stood in the doorway, her hands on her hips.

From out in the kitchen, he could hear the hubbub typical of that time of day. The women were bustling around the kitchen getting supper on the table, and the men were finishing up with chores, coming and going and settling the animals for the night. The house smelled of fresh bread baking and…contentment.

"I see you fetched Mam's cousin." She tilted her head in the direction of the kitchen. When he'd entered the house a few minutes ago, his arms full of firewood, Phoebe was helping prepare supper with his sisters. She had been busy opening canning jars of spiced pears and apples. Rosemary's table was never anything fancy, but the food was always hearty and some of the best he'd ever eaten.

"*Ya*, I picked Phoebe up at the bus station." Joshua stacked two more logs in the wood box to the right of the fireplace. He'd chosen apple wood to burn this evening. It had come from one of the trees he and Jacob had cut down from the old orchard in the far northern corner of the property. He loved the smell of apple wood burning. He thought Phoebe might, too.

"Met her, did you? She's nice," he went on, not waiting for Bay to respond. "Smart, but not too serious. Not full of herself. And kind. She was helping an Englisher lady at the bus station when I got there. Not all girls would do that. Help a stranger. Did you get a chance to talk to Phoebe? Did you like her?"

"Ya." Bay drew out the word. "I liked her well enough. Joshua, I was hoping we could get together today. Maybe after supper, once everything is cleaned up?"

He moved the last of the logs from the pile on a piece of tarp on the floor to the wood box, and then scooted over in front of the fireplace. He thought he'd go ahead and start the fire, so it would be burning well by the time the family gathered together in the living room.

"We'll have to see about that," he hemmed. It wasn't that he wasn't eager to sit down with Bay. He just wasn't sure that tonight was the night for him and Bay to go off on their own. Not with this being Phoebe's first night there. It wouldn't be right for Bay and him not to be with the family. "Might have to be tomorrow. I told Levi that after morning chores, I'd give him a hand clearing out that section of the barn he and Dat are making into a work space for their buggies. But after that…" He gave a nod, indicating there would be time then.

His father had been in the business of making harnesses and other leather goods since he was a young man. That experience had expanded into running a large retail shop here in Delaware. But Benjamin Miller had always had a place in his heart for buggy making. His grandfather had been a buggy maker. Now that he had boys old enough—and trustworthy enough, he teased them—he was interested in trying his hand at building buggies. He planned to build one for his family first, then maybe one for Rosemary's married daughter, Lovage, whose family was growing. Joshua's brother Levi was keen on the idea. Though Levi was a hard worker and good with leather, his heart wasn't in the harness business, so he was eager to get the work space created so he and their father could start their first project.

Bay folded her arms over her chest. "Josh, we need to get all of our hens in a row before we go to your father with our plan. We need to go over the numbers. How much we plan to spend on seeds, how many plants that will yield. What we think we can sell them for—" she ticked off. "Everyone is in the potted plants business. I think we need to consider adding some indoor varieties— indoor plants folks can take in after the growing season. I know there's a risk…"

Joshua nodded, trying to give his sister his full attention and not let his mind wander. But it was hard. He just couldn't stop thinking about Phoebe. And not just about how pretty she was, but how much he liked her. How he'd liked her from the moment he first met her, the moment she'd spoken. Something was calming about her voice, something about her manner that just made him feel… He didn't know how to describe it. She just seemed like no one else he knew. None of the young women he knew, at least. Most girls her age were so flighty and hard to have a real conversation with.

Not that he had a lot of experience with women, not his stepsisters, his age. Sure, he occasionally drove a girl home from a singing, the Amish version of a date. In July he'd taken his friend Caleb Gruber's sister-in-law home from a taffy pull and then a picnic, but it hadn't been anything serious. She'd gone back to Kentucky, and he heard she was courting a blacksmith's son. But none of the girls he'd taken home were as mature as Phoebe. Not that she seemed old to him, though he suspected she was older than him by a year or two. She just seemed wiser than the young women he knew. More levelheaded.

"Do you know how old she is?" Joshua asked suddenly. "Phoebe, I mean." It wasn't until he spoke her name that he realized Bay must have still been talking.

The look on Bay's face left no doubt in his mind. She narrowed her gaze. "If you're not serious about wanting to build this greenhouse and garden shop with me, Josh, you need to tell me now. You need to—"

"No, no," he interrupted, getting to his feet. "Of course I'm serious about it. And I want to add the lean-to onto the barn so we can sell our plants, I just…" He grabbed a bundle of kindling and went back to the fireplace.

"You just what?" Bay asked, taking on a stern tone of voice. She sounded like his older sister Lovey now. Lovey's voice always changed when she became annoyed with someone. "What's got you so preoccupied?" She lowered her voice. "What's the reason for all this talk about Cousin Phoebe?"

He knelt on the redbrick hearth and began to stack the larger pieces of kindling on top of the smaller pieces, taking care to leave plenty of open space between them to allow the fire to breathe. "No…no reason," he said, suddenly feeling self-conscious. He'd never felt this way about a girl the way he thought about Phoebe. Fluttery in his chest. He knew he was attracted to her. He'd been attracted to girls before, but this was different. This wasn't just about a pretty face.

"You know she came here because she had to," Bay intoned.

He concentrated on stacking the wood just right so the fire would catch on the first try. "I don't care about that sort of thing. Men don't care about gossip the way women do."

"Joshua, it's not—" She didn't finish her thought.

Bay was quiet for a moment, quiet long enough that he glanced over his shoulder at her. She was still standing in the doorway. Her arms were crossed over her chest again. She didn't seem pleased with him, but he wasn't exactly sure why. Did she really think he wasn't serious about wanting to build the greenhouse? Sometimes it was hard to know what women were thinking.

Who was he kidding? He almost never knew.

"Fine," she said. "We'll go over the figures tomorrow. Supper's about ready. You'd best wash up. You know how Mam is about coming late to the table."

"Just about done here," he answered, crumpling a piece of newspaper to push beneath the neatly stacked kindling.

He heard her turn to go, then stop in the doorway.

"Joshua," she said softly. "It would be best if you didn't—" She went quiet midsentence again.

"Best I not what?" he asked, looking over his shoulder at her.

She shook her head. "Never mind," she said. "Wash up."

"Ya," he answered, getting to his feet. He needed to

clean up any mess he'd made, and then if he was quick he'd have time to get upstairs and not just wash his hands, but brush his hair, too. And maybe even put on a clean shirt. Not that his shirt was all that dirty, but there was nothing wrong with a man wanting to look his best at his parents' supper table, was there?

"You were looking for me?" Joshua walked into the parlor where Rosemary was sitting on the couch, her foot in the black orthopedic boot, propped on a stool. He had a mug of coffee in his hand, the last from the pot that Tara had insisted he take when he'd cut through the kitchen in search of his stepmother. It was Jesse who had said his *mam* wanted to speak with him.

Rosemary looked up from the sock on her lap that she was darning. "Joshua." She smiled at him and then snipped a thread that ran between the gray sock and her needle with a pair of scissors. "Come in. Fence *ret* up?"

After breakfast, his father had sent him to the corner of the north pasture to repair a sagging fence. It was his father's belief that fences were best mended before the cows got out. It had been cold and windy outside, and Joshua's hands had gotten stiff even though he'd worn work gloves. But he hadn't minded tackling the task alone because it had given him some time to think. With such a large family, time alone wasn't easily found, and he'd welcomed it. He'd spent a bit of time in prayer as he worked, then had run numbers in his head for the plans for the greenhouse. Eventually, his thoughts had drifted to Phoebe. He just couldn't help himself. This morning she'd come down to breakfast not in the black everyday dress she'd been wearing when he'd picked her up at the bus station, but in a blue dress that looked just like one of his sisters' dresses. In fact, he was fairly certain one of them had loaned or given it to her. In the blue dress, Phoebe's eyes had seemed even bluer, her cheeks rosier. And she'd been smiling. *Hockmut*, or *pride* in English, wasn't a good thing among the Amish. He hadn't thought she was being prideful, only that the pretty, calf-length dress with her white apron made her feel happy. And happiness was never discouraged among their people.

"Fence is standing tall again," he told Rosemary, reining in his thoughts. "It was bent coming into our pasture, not going out. Deer maybe? Population's heavy this year and winter has come earlier."

"*Ya*, I've seen them in the field with the horses at sunset." She rolled the mended sock into its mate. "Looking for feed, I suppose."

Joshua sipped from his mug. The coffee had cooled down but was still good. Black and nice and strong the way he liked it. "*Ya*, corn probably," he agreed, feeling awkward. Except for church services, the parlor was more the women's domain than the men's. Especially since Rosemary had had her surgery. "Thought you were allowed to start walking." He pointed to her foot.

"Just resting a bit before dinner. Your father thinks I've been on it too much. A little swelling, nothing more." She gave a wave. "He worries too much." She added the socks to a growing pile on the end table beside her and he watched her fish another pair from a basket at her feet. "I wanted to ask you a favor, Joshua."

He stood a little straighter, slipping one hand into his pocket. He could smell the aroma of roasting turkey wafting from the kitchen. They were having turkey and mashed potatoes and gravy for dinner. With buttermilk biscuits. He couldn't wait. "Sure. What do you need?"

"Edna and John Fisher are having a harvest supper for the young, single folks Friday night. Singing after, I hear. Are you going?"

Joshua raised his coffee mug to his mouth, thinking on the matter. "*Ya*, maybe. I have to see if—"

"*Goot*," she interrupted. "Because I want you to ask Phoebe to go with you."

Joshua had just taken a drink of coffee and the liquid caught in his throat. He coughed, then choked. "I'm sorry—" He covered his mouth with his hand and tried to catch his breath. More coughing followed, and he hoped coffee wouldn't come out of his nose. That would be embarrassing.

"You all right?" Rosemary asked, looking up, concern in her voice.

"Fine," he managed, still coughing. He reached for his handkerchief in his pocket. Gripping the mug in one hand, he used the other to wipe his mouth and then his nose—just to be certain. "You want me to—" He cleared his throat.

"Ask Phoebe to go with you, *ya*." Rosemary was staring at him now.

"Um…"

"I suspect Tara and Nettie are going. And you know Ginger, she wouldn't miss a singing where there are eligible young men for all the cake in the county." She began to thread her darning needle again. "Who can say with Bay. She can be shy around boys her age." She rolled her eyes. "Has no problem telling a customer what's what, though, does she?"

Joshua sniffed and slipped his handkerchief back into his pocket. He blinked the tears from his eyes. Not knowing what to say in response to Rosemary's comment about Bay, he didn't say anything. It was true that Bay wasn't much interested in courting, not the way Ginger was. But he figured Bay was like him, just not ready for that in his life. At least that's what he'd thought until Phoebe arrived. And now...not that he thought she'd ever be interested in him. He'd found out that, as he had suspected, she was two years older than he was. But if she had been interested in him, he could see himself walking out with her. Of course, that would never happen. He kept reminding himself of that.

"Jacob will be going. I hear he's sweet on Lovey's neighbor. And Levi. He never misses a chance to eat." She pushed a beanbag she used for darning into the toe of the sock and began to whipstitch the hole. "It would be nice for Phoebe to be included. You can all ride together."

"Um..." He hesitated, not knowing what to say. He couldn't ask Phoebe to go with him to the singing. What if she thought he meant it as a date? Usually, boys asked girls to ride *home* from singings as a way to spend time alone with them, but what if things were different where she came from? He wouldn't want Phoebe to think he was interested in her.

Or would he?

"Why...you don't think, um...one of the girls should invite her?" he asked, feeling completely off balance.

Rosemary looked up from her darning, meeting his gaze. "I asked you because she likes you."

He held his breath. She *liked* him?

"She's comfortable with you. Besides," Rosemary went on, returning her attention to her darning needle, "I want her to go because Eli Kutz will be there. You know, the widower from Rose Valley. He's chaperoning." She smiled. "And I'm thinking he might make a fine husband for Phoebe."

Phoebe pulled a wet towel from the laundry basket in the muddy grass, gave it a shake and hung it over the clothesline. It was the warmest day they'd had since she arrived in Hickory Grove, and she was glad to have a few moments to herself outside. The sun was shining. The air was crisp with the smell of wood smoke from the house and the fainter smell of apples not yet harvested from the orchard. The downside of the sudden increase in temperatures, however, was that the ice had melted, and it was muddy, meaning she had to take care with the laundry. Anything that touched the grass would be soiled and have to be washed again.

Reaching for a clothespin from the cloth bag hanging on the line, she eyed the woodshed. She'd spotted Joshua going in a few minutes ago, but he hadn't come out. Once, she thought she'd caught a glimpse of him looking around the corner of the building in her direction, but there was no sign of him now. She wondered what he was doing in the woodshed. Organizing, maybe?

Smiling to herself, she grabbed another wet towel. He was a hard worker, that one. And kind. Particularly to her since her arrival. Everyone in the family had, of course, been welcoming. But Joshua was the one who time and time again made the extra effort to make her feel more comfortable in her new surroundings. He always made sure she knew what was going on in the family and how things were done. He did things like seeking her out to tell her what time family prayer took place. He explained to her that his father and brothers all liked their coffee very strong, preventing her from serving the weak coffee her stepfather preferred. He'd also made an effort to make her feel included in the day-to-day activities of the family, whether it meant inviting her to play checkers in the evening or explaining who was who during a lively conversation between his sisters about a new family who had just bought a farm nearby. He was such a thoughtful young man.

Despite missing her John-John so much that it physically hurt, Joshua was the one who made her feel as if coming to Hickory Grove was the right thing to do. And Rosemary and Benjamin's twins. For some reason, the little boys had taken to her immediately and begun asking for her. With Rosemary trying to stay off her feet, and James and Josiah being so active, it had seemed only natural that Phoebe become their nanny of sorts. That was an Englisher word Rosemary had explained to her. It meant a woman who cared for another woman's children. And Phoebe had embraced the job. She had been afraid spending so much time with the toddlers so close in age to her son would make her miss him more, but their sticky hugs and laughter actually eased the ache in her chest for her own child. And reminded her why she was here—to make a better life for herself and for him.

Feeling as if she was being watched, Phoebe looked up to see Joshua standing at the edge of the woodshed. They made eye contact and she smiled. He wasn't wearing his Englisher sunglasses today so she could see his dark eyes. He hesitated, then started toward her. He was wearing a denim barn coat, a knit cap pulled over his head and shoes that were wet and caked with mud.

Phoebe looked down at the clunky knee-high rubber boots she'd borrowed from the laundry room. Bay had told her to find a pair that fit and wear them. She said she did it all the time. Phoebe grabbed a white bedsheet from the laundry basket. She hoped he didn't think she looked foolish, but she'd been afraid if she didn't wear the boots, she might have ended up with mud on the pretty blue dress Tara had given her. Phoebe had never had such a beautiful dress. In her stepfather's home, the women all wore black even though the men wore colored shirts. She hadn't been allowed to have buttons, either, not even hidden in her clothing. That was because women, her stepfather had explained, were far more likely to be drawn into the evils of adornment and couldn't be trusted with blue or green dresses. Or buttons. The idea seemed silly to Phoebe, but no one in their home had ever been interested in her opinions on anything.

That included her belief that wearing a prayer *kapp* wasn't always practical in a busy household, mainly because it had to be kept starched and pristine at all times. Evidently, Benjamin agreed with Phoebe because around his house, Rosemary and her daughters often wore a scarf instead of a prayer *kapp*. A lot of women in their church district did so, Ginger had explained to Phoebe. And then Tara had produced a scarf for indoor use for Phoebe and a heavier wool one for outdoors. The scarf provided modesty, but was also practical.

A sudden gust of wind came up and Phoebe gave a little cry as the bedsheet flew off the line. She grabbed the edge before it hit the grass, but then struggled to get control of it in the wind.

"Need some help?" Joshua called, hustling across the short distance between them.

Phoebe looked up at him through a tangle of white sheet and laughed. "*Ya*, because I'm determined not to get this one dirty again, else it will have to go back in the wash."

Standing on the other side of the clothesline from her, he managed to grab a corner, then a second as the sheet whipped in the wind. "Got it!" He pulled his side down over the line and she did the same on her side.

"Danke." She laughed, taking a handful of wooden clothespins. "A good day for doing laundry with the sunshine," she told him as she clipped one pin after the other to secure the sheet to the line. "But a little tricky with the wind."

He just stood there nodding.

"There we go." She clipped the last clothespin securely.

"There we go," he echoed.

Phoebe studied him standing only inches away on the other side of the sheet on the line. The same way they had stood on either side of the grocery cart that day at Byler's store. Joshua was watching her, which made her feel both at ease and uncomfortable all at the same time. Why was he looking at her that way? As if he'd taken a bite of something and he wasn't sure if he liked it. "Joshua…"

"Ya?" He raised his eyebrows.

"You can let go now."

"Sorry?" He leaned closer to her.

"The sheet." She pointed. "You can let go of it now. It would take a plow horse to rip it loose."

He looked down at his hands resting on the clothesline. "Oh…right." He pulled back and laughed.

"Good of you to help," she said, pushing the laundry basket through the grass with her foot. She pulled a pillowcase from the laundry basket, gave it a shake and started to clip it onto the clothesline.

"Let me give you a hand with that." He grabbed both corners of the top of the pillowcase.

She looked up with surprise. An Amish man who shopped for groceries *and* did laundry? That seemed almost beyond belief. "I can do it."

"I know, but I want to help you."

He shrugged, and she couldn't help but notice how broad his shoulders were. She wondered how old he was. Close to her age, she thought, but she wasn't good at guessing ages. She wondered if he was courting a girl. She didn't think so. Else someone would have mentioned it by now, wouldn't they? Rosemary, one of the girls or Joshua himself?

He held the pillowcase in place on the line. "And doesn't the Bible tell us that two hands are better than one?" he said.

"*Ya*, because they have a good return for their labor."
She smiled at him.

"Proverbs?" he asked.

"Ecclesiastes." The pillowcase secure, she pulled
another from the basket.

"*Ya*, right." He slipped his hands into his pockets
and looked down at his muddy shoes, then back up at
her. "Ah… Phoebe…"

"*Ya?*"

"I wanted to ask you—how are you doing?" he asked,
seeming to suddenly take an abrupt turn in what he had
intended to say.

"How am I *doing*?" His question seemed odd. And
not one she was used to being asked. "Fine." She focused on fastening the pillowcase, feeling uncomfortable again.

"I mean *really*. Are you doing okay? I can't—" He
halted and started again. "I can't imagine what it must
be like to leave your family, your home. Not knowing
anyone here. I've never been away from my father and
brothers for more than a week and that's when I went
to Ohio to see my cousins. I couldn't wait to get back,
I missed them so much," he said.

The tone of his voice took her by surprise. And
touched her at the same time. The emotion, the honesty in his words wasn't something she was used to.
"My family isn't like yours," she said carefully.

He was watching her. "How do you mean?"

She reached into the laundry basket and pulled out
another sheet, and she was thankful to have something
to do with her hands. Suddenly she was feeling overheated and wished she'd left the denim coat she was

wearing unbuttoned. It was also borrowed from the laundry room. "My stepfather is…" She took a breath, glancing away. She looked back at him. "Did you need something?" She changed the subject because she wasn't sure she was up to a discussion of her family. Which would lead to a discussion of her son.

"Um." He stood up straighter, moving stiffly as he helped her hang the last sheet in the basket over the clothesline. "*Ya*, I, um… There's a harvest dinner Friday night at the Fishers. For…you know, unmarried folks. We'll eat and visit, and there will probably be singing. And pie. Edna makes a fine peach pie from her own preserves. And apple. The girls are going, and…and Jacob and maybe Levi." He held the sheet in place for her as another gust of wind came up.

"Sounds nice," she said, not entirely sure why he was telling her about the gathering.

"And I was wondering," he went on. "You're probably not interested, but—" He exhaled and started again. "Don't feel like you have to, I mean, you might think it's boring, but…"

At last, she realized where he was going with his stumbling words. "Are you asking me if I'd like to join you?"

He stared at the sheet between them. "*Ya*, if you… if you'd like."

She smiled at him. She'd never been to a supper for unmarried men and women. Not a singing, either. Other church districts in her county had them. She'd heard it from other girls when she went to the market with her mother. But her stepfather hadn't allowed her or any of her stepbrothers or stepsisters to go. The intention of such gatherings was to let young unmarried folks get to know each other. It was the way young men and women began courting and that led to marriage. At this point in her life, this sort of event wasn't where she would meet the kind of man who would be willing to court her. Or to marry her. But it sounded like such fun. And there hadn't been enough fun in her life.

"*Ya*, I'd like to go," she told Joshua, looking at him.

"You would?" He took a step back, right into a puddle. Realizing what he'd done, he stepped sideways, but it was too late as the water splashed and ran into his shoes.

She shook her head. Men did the oddest things sometimes. How did he not know to choose better footwear on a day like this? "Where are your rubber boots?" she asked, picking up the empty laundry basket.

He looked up sheepishly at her and pointed. "I think maybe on your feet."

They both laughed.

Chapter Four

As the wagon turned into a long driveway, Phoebe shifted on the bench seat and patted the white prayer *kapp* Rosemary had given her. It was a gift, her cousin had insisted. A precious gift to Phoebe not just because of the symbolism of a woman's prayer *kapp*, but because she had never in her whole life received so many heartfelt gifts. It seemed as if every day, in her bedroom in the girls' wing, something new was left on her bed, with its crisp white sheets and finely stitched quilt. There was the blue dress she was wearing, a white apron for everyday use and another for special occasions, a pretty little hair comb and a brush. And this morning she had found a pair of rubber boots that fit her feet... and weren't Joshua's.

The thought made her smile and she looked up to where he was seated on the front plank bench of the wagon, the reins in his capable hands. He was talking to his twin brother, Jacob, seated beside him, but he kept glancing over his shoulder at her. He kept making eye contact. Smiling. They were identical twins, Jacob and Joshua, but she had no difficulty telling them apart because Joshua's eyes lit up each time he looked at her.

Phoebe glanced at Ginger sitting next to her on the middle bench in the wagon. She was chattering nonstop to Nettie and Tara, who were riding on the back bench. The girls were talking about a boy who was supposed to be at the harvest dinner tonight. Someone's cousin. The girls all thought him quite handsome, and Bay was determined to get him to ask her to ride home with him. Ginger was so beautiful with her blond hair and angelic face that Phoebe thought she'd have no trouble convincing this boy from Lancaster to ask her to go with him. In fact, she doubted there would be any man there tonight who could resist her beauty and charm.

The wagon hit a bump in the driveway, jostling them all, and Ginger and her sisters squealed and then burst into laughter. Phoebe held tightly to the side of the wagon to steady herself but remained silent. She liked all of the Stutzman girls and they had been nothing but kind to her, but sometimes she couldn't help but feel the divide between her and them. Losing her John and then giving birth out of wedlock made her feel old, if not in years, then in experience.

"Sorry for that," Joshua threw over his shoulder. "I keep telling Jeb he needs to fill that hole in. Guess I'll have to show up with my own shovel and get it done." He glanced back to Phoebe. "Jeb is one of Edna and John Fisher's sons. I'll introduce you. We're pals."

Phoebe nodded but said nothing. She was so excited she didn't know what to say. Her first singles gathering! She couldn't have been more thrilled if she'd been sixteen. The thought of good food, good company, laughter and song made her heart sing. And according to Joshua, their church district was supportive of their young folks and held these get-togethers regularly. What a beautiful place Hickory Grove would be to raise her John-John.

A buggy pulled into the driveway behind them and an Amish boy leaned out the window, hollering to the Stutzman girls in the back of the wagon. "Yoo-hoo!" he called, pulling off his knit cap and waving it at them.

"Len Troyer!" Ginger shouted, raising up on one knee. She used Phoebe's shoulder to steady herself as she turned to him. "You best get back in that buggy before you take a tumble and fall on your head."

"I'll do it if you promise to ride home with me tonight."

"Early in the evening to already be asking a girl to ride home with you," Nettie shouted to him.

"Say you will, Ginger. Make me a happy man," Len called good-naturedly.

"*Ne*, I'll not say yes yet, Len," Ginger threw back. "What if I get a better offer?"

All four Stutzman girls burst into laughter again.

"I've had enough of this gaggle of geese," Jacob declared from the front bench. And with that, he leaped out of the moving wagon. The moment his boots hit the ground, he cut in front of the wagon and took off running up the driveway.

"It's all meant in good jest. The teasing," Joshua explained to Phoebe, glancing at her. "Want to sit up here?" He patted the place his brother had just vacated.

It only took Phoebe a moment to contemplate the suggestion, and when he offered her his hand, covered in a leather glove, to help her over the front bench, she took it. Managing to keep her balance and not trip over the hem of her cloak, she dropped onto the bench beside him.

The Stutzman girls continued to call back and forth to the young men in the buggy behind them. Now there were two more boys hanging out the windows.

"Len's a good guy," he explained. "Only I'll warn you, no matter what he says, don't agree to let him take you home."

Phoebe felt her cheeks grow warm. She doubted anyone would be asking her to ride home with him tonight or any night. These young men weren't looking for someone like her, a woman with a child and a past. Even if she *had* confessed her sin before God and her congregation and been granted forgiveness. Because forgiveness was something some people found hard to find in their hearts, no matter what the Bible said. That had been evident with her stepfather. And many other folks in her community.

But tonight all of that was far from her mind. Tonight, she was happy and she was going to enjoy every moment of that pleasure. "And why shouldn't I ride home with him?" Phoebe asked, her tone teasing.

Joshua leaned closer so only she could hear him. "He tried to kiss Ginger this summer. *Unsought.*" He raised his eyebrows. "Ginger likes to be silly and have a good time, but she will set a boy straight pretty quick if he tries to take liberties. And she tells everything to anyone who will listen. Len Troyer hasn't been able to get a girl to ride home with him in months." He sat up, then thinking of something else he wanted to say, he leaned close again. "Except Faith King." He grinned.

"But her mother rode home with them. Seated between them in his courting buggy, I heard."

Joshua's smile was infectious, and Phoebe smiled, too, studying his face in the semidarkness. He was dressed like all of the other young men his age: homemade denim britches, boots, a denim coat and a black knit cap. But in her mind, he stood out. And not because she found him handsome. There was just something about him that made her smile every time she laid eyes on him. If she didn't know better, she would have thought she was smitten with him. But was that even possible, after all she had been through? Wasn't she beyond the attractions of youth? She did want to marry of course, partly because it was a woman's duty but mostly because she knew her son needed a father. But it had never occurred to her, not in all the days since her John's death, that she could ever care for another man. The idea intrigued her, and also scared her. Could she truly give her heart to another?

Just then, the canopy of dense tree limbs gave way to an opening. Phoebe's breath caught in her throat as the darkness burst into light with hundreds of twinkling bright lights in the trees beside the farmhouse. "Oh, my," she breathed.

Joshua looked up, nodding in the direction of the strings of lights in two hickory trees that illuminated an area set up with picnic tables. Young women who had arrived earlier were setting up a table of food and stacking plates and laughing and talking together while a cluster of young men stood off to the side, watching them and occasionally calling to them.

"Ah, the Englisher Christmas lights." He pointed

at them. "John Fisher has a thing for them. Buys more every year after Christmas when they go on sale."

"He has *electricity*?" Phoebe asked in awe as she continued to stare at the lights that seemed like bright stars in the dark sky.

"Of course not." Joshua chuckled. "A generator." Pulling gently back on the reins, he slowed the bay and headed toward a two-story barn. There were already six buggies and several wagons parked in front of it. "John can be fancy sometimes, but not *that* fancy. And it took him a full year to convince Bishop Simon to let him have those twinkle lights."

"Our bishop would never have allowed such a thing," she breathed, craning her neck to look at the lights as they rolled past the house and into the barnyard.

"It was John's wife, Edna, who convinced the bishop. There are so many of our communities that are having a hard time getting single folks to come to gatherings like this." He shrugged. "Instead, we find other ways to entertain ourselves. Ways less godly. Less safe. Drinking alcohol and such. Especially boys," he added. "Edna told the bishop that there was no reason why a singing or taffy pull couldn't be godly and still fun. She also pointed out to him that there is nothing in the Bible that forbids twinkle lights." He laughed as he reined in the horse and the wagon rolled to a stop. "And here we are." He sounded almost disappointed now.

Phoebe realized she was, too. Not because they had arrived, but because the wagon ride here was over, and she and Joshua would go their separate ways. Now she had to meet new people. Try to fit in with all these young unmarried folks. Folks who didn't have a little one at home waiting for them.

The buggy behind them pulled in next and half a dozen boys tumbled out, all talking and laughing. Ginger, Tara, Bay and Nettie were out of the wagon at once, walking to the back to fetch the food Rosemary had sent. There was gingerbread and homemade applesauce, as well as three gallons of Benjamin's spiced apple cider.

Phoebe folded her hands in her lap, suddenly so nervous that she wondered if she'd made a mistake agreeing to come. What was she going to say to people? How was she ever going to fit in with them?

"You okay?" Joshua asked.

She looked up at him, biting down on her lower lip. "I'm not used to… Where I come from there aren't many get-togethers like this," she finished lamely.

"You'll be fine. Everyone is keen to meet you," he insisted.

"We've got the applesauce and pies," Ginger called, walking over to Phoebe's side of the wagon. "You want to help us with the food table? I'll introduce you around."

Phoebe hesitated.

"Phoebe's going to help me with the cider," Joshua answered smoothly as he jumped down from the wagon. "You girls go on."

"Ya?" Ginger asked Phoebe, looking up at her.

Phoebe smiled, relieved. Somehow facing the group beside Joshua made it seem less overwhelming. "*Ya*, we'll get the cider and be along," she told Ginger.

"Okay, but be sure to come to find me later." She lowered her voice so only Phoebe could hear her. "Mam wants me to be sure to introduce you to Eli Kutz. He's here helping to chaperone tonight."

"Eli Kutz?" Phoebe asked.

"Widower," Ginger whispered. "And looking for a wife." She nodded as if she and Phoebe shared a secret. Though it really wasn't that big a secret, was it? Wasn't every woman her age looking for a husband?

"Mam's already talked to him about you."

Phoebe knitted her brow. This was the first she had heard of it. "She has?"

"*Ya*, but don't worry. He's a sweet man." Ginger began to back away from her. "And only four children," she added.

Phoebe couldn't resist a chuckle. "Does that make him a bargain?"

Ginger shrugged. "It means he's pretty desperate for a wife."

Phoebe wasn't entirely sure how to take that, but before she could think of a way to ask, one of the young men from the next buggy called to Ginger.

"Ginger, are you coming?"

Ginger glanced over her shoulder at the handsome young man, then back at Phoebe. "Mam said Eli's keen to meet you, so don't let Joshua hog all your time." With that, she turned and hurried off.

"What was Ginger saying?" Joshua asked when his sister was gone.

He walked around to the back of the wagon and Phoebe followed him. "She said not to let you monopolize all my time." She left out the part about Eli, though why she wasn't quite sure.

He sighed and handed her one of the plastic jugs of

apple cider. "And what did you say to that? Because I was kind of hoping you'd let me walk you around and introduce you."

Phoebe pressed her lips together, not sure how to respond. Did she tell him what she was thinking? It would be forward of her, but also honest.

She looked up at him, meeting his gaze. "Do you have a girl?"

He shook his head.

She felt her heart give a little trip and suddenly her mouth felt dry. Was she *really* falling for him? "Sweet on someone?"

He tilted his head one way and then the other, as if running the idea around in his mind. "You could say that."

Against her will, Phoebe felt a tightening in her throat. An overwhelming sense of disappointment. She looked down at the grass at her feet, illuminated by all of the twinkling lights in the trees. "Then you should go be with her."

He was quiet so long that at last she looked up at him and found him studying her.

"I can't," he said very quietly.

She held his gaze, feeling a little light-headed. She remembered this feeling. She'd felt it in those early days and months when she and John had courted. She nibbled on her lower lip. "Why not?" she dared.

He hesitated, then shrugged. "Because I'm already with her."

Joshua's sweet words made Phoebe suddenly feel weak-kneed. And a little flustered. She glanced away, then back at him. She was too old for the games young people sometimes played. She'd been through too much. She was flattered that he liked her, that he would have the courage to say so. But she was also cautious. Because it was becoming obvious to her that she was sweet on him, too. And because her immediate thought was that he deserved someone better than her. A man like this Eli who Ginger had mentioned was more the type of man to marry a woman like her. "You don't know me, Joshua."

"I know you well enough to know I like you, Phoebe. More than I've ever liked a girl before." He held his hand, palm out, to her. "Don't say anything." He shook his head. "You don't have to say anything. I just… I wanted you to know that. I wanted to—"

"Josh! Are you coming with that cider or not?"

Phoebe looked up to see Jacob standing a few feet away, his arms opened wide. "Edna's waiting on the cider."

"Coming," Phoebe called. She glanced at Joshua and smiled. "We're coming." And then, they walked side by side toward the others in a comfortable silence.

Joshua entered the cozy kitchen that smelled of cinnamon and nutmeg and stewed pumpkin. In his arms, he carried two cases of quart-sized Ball jars he'd brought up from the cellar.

"I appreciate your help fetching those for us," Rosemary told Joshua as he walked in. "I hate to take you from your chores. I know your father had a whole lot of things for you to do this morning."

"I don't mind," he told her. "I'm glad you asked me."

Rosemary was seated at the end of the kitchen table,

folding bath towels. From there, she was able to direct Tara, Bay, Nettie and Phoebe through the process of canning stewed pumpkin and the last of the fresh cabbage they'd been storing in the cellar. His little brothers were playing happily with several pots and pans, wooden spoons and an old tin pie plate in the hallway near the kitchen door. They were free to play anywhere, but under the watchful eye of all the women, they'd be less likely to get into mischief.

"I couldn't find the lids, though," Joshua confessed. "Sorry. I looked everywhere on those shelves where you said they might be."

"I know they're there, but I can't say where," Rosemary fussed, rising from her chair. She began to stack the towels in a laundry basket neatly. "Everything is a hodgepodge around this house these days. Nothing in its place. After being off my feet all this time, I feel like I'll never get caught up."

"I can go down and have another look," Joshua offered, feeling bad that he hadn't been able to find them. With the big orthopedic boot Rosemary was wearing, she shouldn't be going up and down steep cellar steps.

"*Ne*, no need. When can a man ever find anything?" Rosemary asked good-naturedly. "This morning your father asked me where the toothpaste was. On the sink, of course, next to his toothbrush." She chuckled. "*Ne*, no need for you to go back to the cellar. One of the girls can run down and have a look. They're probably on a different shelf than they're supposed to be."

"Spice or no spice in this batch of pumpkin, Mam?" Nettie called from the stove, where she was dumping a large bowl of raw pumpkin pieces into a pot.

"Just set the jars there on the table," Rosemary instructed Joshua, pointing. Then to Nettie, she said, "What was the last batch?"

"Cinnamon, nutmeg, allspice, ginger and clove," Phoebe answered, placing two-pint jars into a divided cardboard box so that each jar had its own niche.

"Then no spice. But be sure to mark the jars," Rosemary warned, scooping a stack of plastic measuring cups up off the end of the table. She crossed the kitchen to hand them to her toddlers. "Here you go, sweets. Make your *mam* some pumpkin pie."

"Dank-ee!" James squealed.

Josiah echoed a word less comprehensible but most definitely the English version of *thank you*.

"You're welcome," Rosemary told the boys.

Unlike most Amish households, his father and stepmother had decided their little ones would learn both English and Pennsylvania *Deutsch* from birth. Generally, Amish children only spoke *Deutsch* at home and didn't learn English until they went to school at six years old. It tickled Joshua to hear his little brothers already babbling in both languages.

Joshua was half tempted to drop to the floor and "make a pie" with them, but he knew he should head outside. He had plenty to do. In an hour, he was supposed to take a shift at the cash register in the harness shop, relieving Ginger, and before that, he needed to check the latch on the chicken coop. Tara had told him this morning at the breakfast table that it was sticking again, and she was concerned it might not latch properly. An open chicken coop at night in cold weather was an invitation to every fox in the county. Only a week ago one of their customers at the harness shop had lost a dozen guinea hens to the pesky marauders when one of their children had accidentally left the coop door open all night.

"Phoebe, did I tell you," Nettie said from the sink, "that Eli Kutz was at the shop yesterday asking about you?"

"Was he?" Phoebe asked, her back to Nettie.

"He said he enjoyed talking with you at the harvest supper. I think he was hoping to catch you at the shop. He asked if you ever worked the register."

Joshua couldn't tell by Phoebe's tone of voice if she was interested. He knew his stepmother thought Eli would be a good fit for Phoebe, but that didn't mean Phoebe agreed with her. He'd seen her and Eli talking at the harvest supper, but she hadn't mentioned Eli to him. Of course, it didn't surprise him that Eli would be interested. Why wouldn't he be, a woman as pretty as Phoebe? As smart and fun.

Not really wanting to hear any more about Eli, Joshua wandered over to the stove and breathed in the aroma of the nearest kettle. "Smells good," he told Phoebe. "We having pumpkin pie for dessert after supper by any chance? Looks like there's enough still left in the pot."

Phoebe wiped another jar of freshly packed pumpkin and slid it into the box. "Nettie made up the crust this morning after breakfast."

"Excellent. I hope you're making half a dozen pies, because I can eat one all by myself." He started to lower his finger into the simmering pot of pumpkin, but Ginger tapped his hand with a wooden spoon.

"Out of that or there won't be pie."

"It doesn't taste good yet, anyway," Nettie warned him, fishing a hot quart-sized Ball jar from a pot of boiling hot water with a pair of tongs. She set the jar carefully on a tray on the counter and fished out another. "No sugar or milk added yet."

"But there's some cooked cabbage if you're hungry," Phoebe suggested.

Bay picked up the tray of hot canning jars and moved them to the counter beside the stove. "Don't encourage him, Phoebe." She eyed her brother. "He can wait for supper. You feed him one bowl of cabbage and all those boys will be in here wanting a bowl. You don't know how much they can eat. Or what a mess they will make in this kitchen in the midst of our canning."

Joshua wrinkled his nose, contemplating scooping a little of the pumpkin out and adding sugar. It just smelled so good with all those spices. "Don't like cabbage much."

"No?" Phoebe wiped the lid of another jar. "Me, either. Unless I add a little red wine vinegar."

"Vinegar?" Realizing he was still wearing his knit cap, Joshua pulled it off and slipped it into his coat pocket. Then he wondered how bad his hair looked and ran his fingers through it.

Since the harvest dinner, he and Phoebe had been spending quite a bit of time together. It just seemed like they clicked. He always had something to tell her and found himself trying to steal moments here and there to be alone with her. And if he didn't know better, he would think she'd been doing the same. He'd been really nervous after telling her he was sweet on her that night, but he was beginning to think maybe she felt the same way about him.

Or was that too much to hope for? What if she had taken to Eli Kutz the same way he had apparently taken to her? He wondered if he should ask one of his stepsisters to try to feel Phoebe out. See if she liked him or was just being polite, but somehow that didn't seem right to him. All the young women he knew were always gossiping about this boy or that, who they liked, who they didn't, but that seemed to him like games he didn't want to play anymore.

Joshua looked at Phoebe. "I never thought of putting vinegar on it."

She lifted one shoulder and let it fall. "You should try it."

"Oh, goodness," Rosemary exclaimed. "Who is that smelling up my kitchen?" She leaned down and tickled James at the nape of his neck. "Is that you, my little chick?"

The boy giggled, and then Josiah leaned down to get his mother to tickle him.

"Phew wee!" Rosemary went on dramatically. "Someone needs a diaper change." She leaned down to pick Josiah up.

"Mam! You shouldn't be carrying him up those stairs. He's too heavy."

"I can take them up to change them," Phoebe offered.

"*Ne*, I'll do it." Tara wiped her hands on a dish towel and crossed the kitchen toward her mother. "Give him here." She took her little half brother. "And what about you, you little skunk?" She reached down and swung James into her arms. "Are you ready for a diaper change?"

Rosemary kissed the back of the closest little boy's head and Joshua smiled. In a lot of Amish homes, there weren't such displays of affection. He didn't know any family that didn't love their children, but he liked the way his father and Rosemary were so demonstrative in their fondness. He thought he'd be the same way with his own children someday. If God blessed him with children. With a wife. He glanced at Phoebe.

"I'll be right back," Tara called. "Just as soon as we get these skunks' diapers changed." She glanced at Phoebe. "If that case of pumpkin is ready to go to the cellar, could you take it down, and then check to see if you can find those lids? I know we bought more from Byler's last month when they went on sale."

"I think I saw them," Phoebe called after Tara as she and Rosemary and the boys went down the hall. "I'll find them." She glanced at Joshua and smiled, and then picked up the case of pumpkin. "Be right back."

Joshua considered offering to carry the case down. Or better yet, following her down. Maybe they could catch a few minutes together. He and Bay had been discussing selling a few plants that were good for building hedges and windbreaks, and he wanted to talk to Phoebe about it. She'd had some really good ideas when they'd talked the other day about his greenhouse. And she hadn't been shy about telling him when she didn't think his ideas were good. Or at least profitable.

"I'll help you look," Nettie offered. "I want to see how well we're set for summer squash. I was thinking about throwing a jar in the soup for supper tonight."

Joshua watched his sister and Phoebe leave the kitchen and then pulled his hat out of his pocket. "Guess I should get something done before my shift in the shop."

"Mmm," Bay said, turning to him. She sighed, leaning against the counter as she crossed her arms over her waist. It was obvious she had something to say to him.

He waited.

Bay glanced at the floor and then back up at him. "I've noticed you and Phoebe are spending a lot of time together."

"We are?" He looked away. "*Ne,* not really."

"I see you talking with her on the back porch, in the yard, on the walk home from church. And I just—"

"You what?" Joshua asked.

"I—" She exhaled again. "You seem sweet on her, Josh." She narrowed her gaze. "Does it not matter to you that her parents sent her away?"

He shrugged. "*Ne.* Parents have disagreements with adult children sometimes. Her stepfather is a harsh man. He's never treated her kindly. He's not like my father, who loves you and your sisters as much as he loves us. Not all families are like ours, Bay."

She raised an eyebrow. "You don't care what she did? The situation she—"

"Stop!" he interrupted, holding up his hand to her. "I won't hear idle, women's gossip, Bay. 'Do not let unwholesome talk come from our mouths,'" he quoted from Ephesians. "You know how Dat feels about that."

She turned back to the stove, picking up a wooden spoon to stir the pieces of pumpkin in the pot. She adjusted the flame beneath it. She seemed upset. "What she did, it's not idle gossip, Josh. Ask Mam or your father, if you don't believe me. If you think I would lie about such a terrible thing."

He felt short of breath. What was Bay talking about? What terrible thing could Phoebe have done that Bay would think it would change his feelings for her?

Weeks ago he had heard something about Phoebe coming to stay with them in Hickory Grove because of a scandal, but he'd assumed it was over something silly. And once he had gotten to know Phoebe better and learned something of her upbringing, he'd been even surer of it. Her stepfather was a harsh man. Strict and inflexible. A man like that could send a daughter to stay with a cousin for any number of reasons. It happened all the time. It was a good way for men and women of marrying age to find spouses outside their own community.

Joshua stared at his boots. "I don't think you're lying to me, Bay. It's only that I—" He what? He took a breath and exhaled slowly.

"It's not that I don't like Phoebe." Bay set down the wooden spoon and walked over to him, her arms crossed over her waist. "But I don't think you should—" She halted midsentence. "I think you should ask her about it. Before you—"

"Before I what?" he demanded, looking up to meet her gaze.

"Before you fall in love with her," she said softly.

Too late, he thought. But he didn't say it. Instead, he turned away. "I better get going." He walked out of the kitchen and out the back door.

Ask her. Bay's words were still echoing in Joshua's

ears as he walked toward the chicken coop in the barn-yard, his head down. Phoebe was such a faithful woman. He couldn't believe she could have done something so terrible that it would matter to him.

But now Joshua was torn. Maybe Bay was right. Maybe he *should* ask Phoebe about it. Get the story from her.

Or would it better to wait for her to tell him about it? Phoebe was just beginning to trust him. If she had something to tell him, she'd tell him in her own good time, wouldn't she?

Reaching the chicken house, he jiggled the latch, testing it.

Ya, he thought to himself. That was the right thing to do. To let her come to him. To let her tell him in her own good time. And she would tell him when she was ready. He was sure of it.

Chapter Five

"'I exhort therefore, that, first of all, supplications, prayers, intercessions, *and* giving of thanks, be made for all men,'" Benjamin read from a worn leather-bound Bible.

As he read, Phoebe clasped her hands in the folds of her black dress and tried to concentrate on God's words and not the rumbling of her stomach. Or the letter lying upstairs on her dresser.

She was hungry because Benjamin's family fasted on Thanksgiving. The good news was that after this final time of prayer and contemplation, the twenty-four-hour fast would end and they would share a meal together. In truth, her empty stomach was far less a concern to her than the letter she'd received from her mother the day before.

The letter had begun pleasantly enough with ordinary news of the goings-on of the household: her mother had started making a new quilt, her eldest stepbrother had become betrothed to the neighbor's pious daughter, Azubah, and the family butchered two hogs for the

coming winter. Her mother had then moved on to news
of Phoebe's son, John-John. The toddler had taken to
a black-and-white kitten in the barn, and he was now
counting to six without making a single mistake.

The letter had then gone on to say that in Phoebe's
absence, John-John had begun calling his grandfather
vadder. The thought of her son calling Edom Wickey
Father had made Phoebe so angry that she'd had to take
a moment to pray for guidance. Then her anger had
turned to fear. When she left home, her intention had
been clear: to find a suitor and return for John-John.
What reason would her stepfather have for allowing
her son to call him Father when he knew that Phoebe
intended to marry and take John-John with her? Edom
knew Phoebe's husband would become her son's father.

Phoebe wanted to believe it was all innocent. Maybe
John-John heard the other children in the house calling Edom *vadder* and he'd copied them. But if that was
true, why had her mother made a point to mention it?
Phoebe knew that Edom read all correspondence that
left the house before it was mailed. That included not
only letters that Phoebe and her older stepsiblings wrote
but her mother's, as well. Had it been a secret warning
from her mother, disguised as newsy chat?

She sighed and opened her eyes.

Just as in church on Sundays, Benjamin and Rosemary's family had gathered with the males on one side
of the living room and the females on the other. The
little ones, James and Josiah, wandered back and forth
between their brothers and sisters and mother while
Benjamin stood before the group in front of the fireplace. Phoebe gazed first at the bowed heads of the

girls covered with prayer *kapps*, then past them to the men's side.

Joshua was watching her.

"'I will therefore that men pray everywhere, lifting up holy hands, without wrath and doubting,'" Benjamin continued, his baritone voice steady.

Joshua caught Phoebe's gaze. He didn't smile, but his eyes twinkled, making her want to smile.

They hadn't had any time to talk today. And she wanted to speak with him, to tell him about the letter from her mother. She didn't know who else she could discuss it with. She had considered speaking to Rosemary because she respected her opinion, but her cousin was so busy with the house and her large family. And though her recovery was going as her doctor expected, she was still healing from her surgery. Phoebe didn't want to burden her with her own troubles. It didn't matter anyway because she hadn't had time to speak to anyone. After morning chores, they'd gathered for prayer and readings from the Bible. After an hour break to check on the animals and see to personal matters, they'd gathered again. There had been another short break at two o'clock when a hearty chicken stew had been put on the woodstove to simmer, and now they were gathered for final prayers before supper.

Joshua smiled now at Phoebe, and she had to close her eyes to prevent herself from smiling back. She loved the little shiver of happiness she felt when he looked at her and when they talked. But it also made her nervous. She knew Joshua had feelings for her. What she didn't know was where she wanted it to lead. Where it *could* lead. Did he think she was the kind of woman he would marry, or was she just a dalliance? He'd admitted to her that he had never had a girlfriend before. Was he too young to consider marriage yet? Was he too young to be ready to commit to the responsibility of marriage? He seemed mature for his age to her, but what if her opinion was influenced by these flutters in the pit of her stomach? What if she was allowing her attraction to him to cloud her logic?

Benjamin indicated they should all bow their heads in a final silent prayer, and Phoebe forced herself to focus on thoughts of thanksgiving for God's gifts and not herself. Within minutes, Benjamin ended the afternoon with encouraging words to uplift his family's spirits, and Rosemary shooed the women into the kitchen to get supper on the table. Now that the fast was over, everyone was eager to eat.

"Pop those biscuits in the oven," Rosemary told Tara as she slowly made her way toward the kitchen, limping in the orthopedic boot she was still wearing. "Nettie and Bay, can you see to setting the table?"

As the women all made their way toward the kitchen, the men went their way, headed to the barns to feed the animals before they broke their fast.

"Fifi!"

Phoebe looked down to see little James tugging on her dress. He raised his chubby hands to her, indicating she should pick him up.

"Oh, goodness," she said, seeing that his hands were covered in something sticky. "Looks like you need a little hand washing, *ya*?" While the adults all fasted, it was not required of the children, and they had eaten snacks throughout the day. "Is that jam?" she teased, lifting the toddler into her arms. "Josiah? Where did you get to?" With James in her arms, she searched for him as the living room emptied.

"This Josiah?" Joshua appeared at Phoebe's side. "Were you looking for this pup?" he asked, jostling his little brother playfully.

Josiah giggled and then James wiggled in her arms.

"Did Bay say anything to you about going out for greenery tomorrow?" Joshua asked. He raised Josiah in the air. "Well, tomorrow or Saturday, depending on the weather."

She shook her head. "No one mentioned it."

"It's a family tradition. We used to do it when we lived in New York. Our family and Rosemary's. Her husband was my father's good friend. Our families went out together every year. We'd gather greenery, you know, mistletoe and pine, and take it home to decorate the shop and our houses and such." He lowered Josiah to his hip, and the toddler tried to climb onto his shoulder. "We usually wait until into December, but Bay and I were thinking we'd make wreaths and garland and try to sell them at the harness shop."

"Sounds like a great idea to me," Phoebe replied, gently extracting the string of her prayer *kapp* from James's hand.

"Anyway, I wondered if you'd like to go with us." He lowered his voice, though there was no one near to overhear them but the two little boys. "We might get a little time alone. I thought a walk in the woods might be nice. Especially with the little bit of snow we got last night."

"I don't know. I'd like to, but I'll have to talk to Rosemary and see if she can spare me. She might need me to keep an eye on these two." She poked her finger into James's tummy. "Who can be a handful."

James giggled and poked her in the shoulder.

"I'd really like it if you could go with us," Joshua said, meeting her gaze.

"Phoebe?" Rosemary called from around the corner, in the kitchen. "Do you have the little rascals?"

"I do! Coming," she returned. She turned to Joshua again. "And why would you like me to go with you?" she asked playfully, feeling saucy. She started for the kitchen and he fell into step behind her.

Joshua leaned over her shoulder and whispered in her ear. "You know very well why. Because I like you, Phoebe. Because I want you to be my girl."

His words startled her almost as much as the sight of Eli Kutz just walking in the back door to the kitchen. In his arms, he carried a little girl about the same age as James and Josiah. She suspected the child was his youngest. She remembered because he'd made a point of saying his daughter needed a mother. What on earth was Eli doing here? Thanksgiving was generally a private day for families.

"I hope I haven't come too early," Eli said to Benjamin.

Phoebe glanced over her shoulder at Joshua. "We'll talk later," she whispered as she entered the kitchen.

"You're certainly not early." Benjamin patted Eli on the back affectionately with one meaty hand. "Just finished with family prayer. Come in, come in." He waved him in. "Rosemary and I are glad you could join us for supper."

"Eli's come for supper?" Phoebe whispered to Ginger.

Ginger took James from her and into her arms and shifted him to her hip. "I think Mam invited him," she murmured so no one else would hear. "She saw him at Spence's Bazaar Tuesday." She raised her eyebrows. "Nettie said he jumped at the invitation. Made a point of asking if you'd be here."

"Me?" Phoebe breathed, purposely not looking in Eli's direction. At first, she'd thought it was kind of Rosemary to be keeping an eye out for possible suitors for her. Now, however, she didn't know how she felt about it. Now that her feelings for Joshua were rising to the surface.

Ginger shrugged. "I guess you made a good impression at the harvest supper."

"Have a seat at the table. The boys are just going out to feed up. We'll be eating soon," Benjamin told Eli jovially. "And who is this little miss?" He tugged on the hem of the little girl's mauve dress. She was dressed identically to other women in the house in a dress, prayer *kapp* and apron, and looked adorable.

Eli bounced his daughter in his arms. "This is my Lizzy. Aren't you?" he asked. He met Benjamin's gaze. "My youngest. Named after my dear wife."

"You've been through a lot, haven't you?" Benjamin's tone was kind. "Well, it's good to have you here with us. Did you bring the other children?"

"The boys are such a handful. They stayed home with my mother." Eli's gaze strayed to Phoebe and he nodded. "Good to see you again, Phoebe."

Phoebe froze, at once feeling awkward. She'd practically been flirting with Joshua a moment ago, and now here was another man who was clearly interested in her.

It didn't seem right to her. She swallowed and nodded, avoiding eye contact with him. "Good to see you, Eli."

Eli was a good six inches taller than she was. Maybe ten years older. She wouldn't have called him handsome. His hair was thinning, his red beard already threaded with gray. But he had kind blue eyes. She'd noticed them the night she'd met him at the Fishers'. They'd shared a pleasant conversation about the weather in Delaware compared to the weather in Pennsylvania, and he'd told her a little bit about his children. He'd shared a sweet story about his middle boys trying to train one of their goats to lie down on command like the family dog. She'd found him easy to talk to. And gentle. He seemed like just the sort of man she had been looking for when she left home.

So why was she feeling distressed to see him here?

"Phoebe," Benjamin called. "Could you get some coffee for Eli and me?" He pulled a chair out at the head of the kitchen table. "Sit, Eli."

"I don't want to keep you from your chores," Eli said, hanging back.

"I wasn't going to the barn," Benjamin assured him. "That's what I have sons for. Sit, sit." He indicated a chair next to him. "You'll take a cup of coffee with me, won't you?" He looked to Phoebe. "Coffee?"

"*Ya*, of course." Phoebe practically tripped over her own feet as she made her way to the stove, where an old-fashioned percolator sat, fresh coffee gurgling in it.

Ginger leaned in toward her as Phoebe went by. "Eli's all eyes for you. I wouldn't be surprised if he asks you to walk out with him."

Phoebe cut her eyes at Ginger as she reached for two

sturdy white coffee mugs from an open shelf against the wall.

Ginger giggled and walked away, still carrying her little brother.

With a sigh, Phoebe poured the coffee. She could feel Eli watching her, even with her back to him. But Joshua had just asked her to be his girl and the moment he said it, she knew it was what she wanted. So having Eli here now put her in a bit of a pickle. What would she do if Eli did ask her to walk out with him? She couldn't say yes, not when she had feelings for Joshua. Feelings he shared with her.

"Here you go," she said, turning to the two men at the far end of the table. "Hot and fresh." She forced a half smile. All she had to do was be nice to Eli, she told herself. Give the men their coffee and then she could busy herself with the meal. She wouldn't even have to speak to him, and then he wouldn't have the chance to ask her to walk out with him. The kitchen was buzzing with activity as Rosemary gave out orders and the girls all hurried to get supper on the table. With all of this confusion, it would be easy enough to avoid the widower.

She set one mug down in front of Eli, carefully still avoiding eye contact. Then she put the other mug down in front of Benjamin. But just as she set it down, Benjamin rose from his chair. "I almost forgot. I need to run down to the barn and check on that yearling calf of mine that's been feeling poorly."

He looked to Phoebe, who realized a second too late that she'd made the mistake of making eye contact with *him*. "Have a seat, Phoebe. Talk with Eli while I run down to the barn."

Before she could protest, Benjamin was practically pushing her into his chair. Phoebe had no choice but to sit, and the next thing she knew, she was eye to eye with Eli.

"Have my coffee," Benjamin told Phoebe. He chuckled. "I've had enough for the day, anyway."

Phoebe didn't even like coffee, but she reached for the warm mug, just to have something to do with her hands.

"Nice of Rosemary to invite me for supper," Eli said, moving his daughter from one knee to the other so that she was no longer between him and Phoebe. From his pocket, he removed a little hand-carved wooden sheep. "Look what your *dat* found," he said in Pennsylvania *Deutsch.*

The little girl closed her hand over the toy and glanced shyly at Phoebe.

"Do you know what a sheep says, Lizzy?" Phoebe asked in the same language. "Baa." she said, imitating the sound.

The little girl giggled.

"It's nice to be here." Eli reached for his coffee mug, the hanging oil lamp over the table casting shadows across his face. "This house is always so lively. It feels like a home. Since Elizabeth passed, my house—" He hesitated. "It's missing a woman's warmth. My mother tries, but—" He exhaled. "It's not the same."

Phoebe kept her attention focused on the coffee in her hand and blew on the surface. Her heart went out to Eli. It was obvious he was lonely and she understood loneliness. She'd experienced her share of it since her betrothed's death. Eli and Phoebe had talked some about his wife, and she had gathered that while there was no romantic love between them, he had loved her as a man loves a woman who cares for his home and has given him children.

As for this house, it was lively, all right. At this moment in the kitchen, Bay and Tara were arguing over whether or not to add dried basil to the chicken stew, James was crying to be picked up again, and a tabby cat had taken up residence in the chair at the far end of the table and was meowing loudly. After setting a lid down on a pot with a clatter, Rosemary lifted the back of the chair, and the cat slid unceremoniously to the kitchen floor and shot under the table.

"Jesse!" Rosemary called. "That cat is in the kitchen again. Take care of her or she'll end up in that stew."

Giggling, her eleven-year-old son scooped the cat up in his arms and hurried out of the kitchen. "No one likes cat in a stew," he said to no one in particular.

Phoebe took a sip of the hot black coffee. "Oh," she said suddenly, half rising up out of the chair. "Eli, can I get you cream for your coffee?"

"Ne," he said, watching her.

"Sugar, then?" she asked, feeling flustered. "The coffee is strong. Benjamin likes it strong."

"Ne." Eli laughed. "Phoebe, sit down. The coffee is fine. I like it black, but I didn't come for the coffee."

She took another sip, and realizing she couldn't possibly drink it, she set the mug down. If she did manage to drink it, she'd be up all night, it was so strong. "You... you didn't?" she asked, switching to English. This was worse than she had even anticipated. He sounded so sweet.

"*Ne*. You know why I'm here." He lowered his voice. "I came to see you."

She stared at the table. This was just what she had hoped for when she'd come to Hickory Grove. Eli was more than what she had hoped for. He was a widower with children in need of a wife. But he was also kind, a hard worker, a faithful man. The night she had met him, she had even thought him to be fun. Especially for a man his age, a man who had suffered the loss of his wife and now had four little ones to care for alone. But he wasn't what she wanted now.

She pressed her lips together, staring at the table.

He took a sip of his coffee. "Truth is, I came to ask you if I might court you. I'm just trying to get up the nerve." He grinned. "Guess I just did."

She swallowed hard, looking away. "I…" She exhaled, not knowing what to say. Not knowing what she *should* say. She and Joshua had no agreement. He'd only brought up her being his girl five minutes ago. But the thing was, she already, in a way, felt as if she was his girl. And even if she wasn't—even if Joshua was mistaken in his feelings for her—Phoebe couldn't, in good conscience, agree to walk out with Eli. Not when she had so many emotions tied to Joshua right now.

"It's kind of you to ask, Eli." She made herself look at him. "I've enjoyed our conversations at the Fishers' and when we ran into each other at Spence's the other day. You're a nice man, but…" She held his gaze. "I don't think— I'll have to say no."

Eli sat back in his chair, his daughter still on his knee. Lizzy slid the wooden sheep across the table, pretending to make it drink from her father's cup.

Eli took a long moment before he said anything. "I'm sorry to hear that. Of course you've just arrived and—" He shrugged. "You're thinking maybe you'll get a better offer," he said, not sounding in the least bit upset. "A young woman as pretty as you are, I imagine you'll have lots of offers."

She shook her head. "You don't know me. You don't know what I've done."

He smiled slowly, a warm, gentle smile. When he spoke it was loud enough for only her to hear him. "If you're talking about your son, Rosemary already told me."

Phoebe sat back in her chair. "She did?" she asked. But of course everyone in the town had to know, didn't they? Everyone in this household had to know. Surely they had told others. And if Rosemary was speaking of her to Eli, she would have been responsible for telling him.

"We've all made mistakes and the Lord forgives us for those mistakes, once we ask forgiveness. I would never judge you, Phoebe."

Tears sprang suddenly to her eyes. "You're a good man, Eli."

"I hope that I am." He lifted one shoulder and lowered it. "Some days I'm better than others." He was quiet for a moment and then went on, "Why not think on it? I want you to know, though, that if we courted, it would be with the intention of marrying. As long as we got on, and I think we would."

Again, she made herself look at him. "I don't know what to say."

"Say nothing. I ask nothing more of you now." He

pushed his mug toward her. "Except maybe a little more coffee."

She smiled, and half wished it was Eli she had dreamed of last night and not Joshua.

The midday sun shone bright overhead and Phoebe lifted her face to savor the warmth. First they'd had snow, then days of rain, and now at last the sun was shining again. "Cold out," she commented, walking beside Bay down the deer path through the woods.

In the distance, Joshua and Jacob walked, their heads together as they carried on a conversation. They were too far away for Phoebe to hear what they were talking about. She wondered if they were talking about her. She and Joshua hadn't been alone to talk about what he had said to her on Thanksgiving Day about wanting her to be his girl. She was half afraid maybe he had changed his mind, because that had been days ago.

They'd come to the woods on the edge of the family farm to harvest greenery. Originally it had been planned for Friday or Saturday, but after the rain all weekend, this was the first opportunity they'd had to go since the woods had dried out a bit. The wagon already had a pile of willow and birch twigs on it, as well as one of white pine and blue spruce branches. They'd left it back on the road they'd come in on. They were now in search of mistletoe, which grew in big balls high in the treetops, particularly oaks. Jacob said he was certain he'd seen mistletoe in the direction they were walking. He carried a rifle on his shoulder, and when they located the holiday greenery he would shoot it down from the tree.

Phoebe clasped her hands together and lowered

her head as the treetops overhead shaded her from the warmth of the sun. She was thankful for the navy-colored wool mittens she had brought with her. They had been her mother's once, and darned many times, but she was comforted by the idea that her mother had once worn them. And she had made an identical pair for her son before she left, thinking they would keep him warm in her absence. The thought of her son suddenly made her miss him so much that she ached for him. It had been three weeks since she'd held him in her arms or kissed the top of his blond head.

"*Ya*, it's cold," Bay agreed. "It was good that we left James and Josiah home. It might have nice for them to take a walk and I know they would have enjoyed riding through the woods in the wagon, but it's too cold out here today for them. Too windy, and James already has a runny nose."

Phoebe nodded, forcing herself not to dwell on how much she missed her little boy. "Benjamin said it might snow again tonight." She breathed deeply, taking in the scent of the pine needles scattered on the forest floor. "I don't smell snow, but it was sure cold enough this morning when we woke."

"I'm glad it held off long enough for us to get out here. I've already sold half a dozen wreaths at the shop just with the sample I made up. Presale," Bay explained. "I hung the one on the door with a little For Sale sign and folks are asking where they can get one."

Phoebe halted as a rabbit raced across the path in front, then started forward again. "It was smart to hang it on the door. I really liked the pine cones you added. How did you get them to stick? Wire?"

Bay held up a low-hanging branch over their heads so they could safely continue. "Glue gun."

"Glue gun?" Phoebe asked. She'd never heard of such a thing.

"It's electric so I have to run it at the shop off the generators, but you put hard glue sticks in and it melts them. It makes it easy to attach pine cones or acorns, even bows. Benjamin's given me a whole bench to work on the wreaths. And," Bay added, "he brought me an armful of trimming from the apple trees in case I wanted to do something with them. I'm thinking the kind of wreath that isn't fresh, so it won't die," she explained.

Phoebe shook her head in wonder. Bay certainly knew a lot about the things Englishers would buy and how to sell them. The idea of building a greenhouse and selling vegetable plants and flowers had been Bay's idea, Joshua had told her. She'd had just invited him to join in the venture, knowing the work at the harness shop wasn't really in his heart. "I think you and Joshua are going to be very successful with this greenhouse and shop you're going to build. Especially if you keep coming up with things like these wreaths to sell." She thought for a moment. "Have you thought about making table arrangements? Like for Christmas. I saw someone selling them at a market once in Pennsylvania."

"What a great idea!" Bay said. "Do you think you could show me what it would look like?"

"*Ya*, I could even make one, I think," Phoebe told her. "Josh keeps asking me to come down to the harness shop. Maybe I could make myself useful."

"I think that's a great idea." Bay glanced at Phoebe. "Phoebe—" She went quiet.

"Ya?" Phoebe fell into step beside Bay.

"I'm just going to come out and say this." She chewed on her lower lip. Her cheeks were wind chapped, and her nose was red. She wasn't as pretty as Ginger, but like all the Stutzman girls, she was awfully pretty. "Know I don't say it to hurt you, only to protect my brother. Stepbrother," she corrected, waving her hand as if to say, *You know what I mean.* She was wearing black work gloves like the ones the men wore. "I hope you're not playing with Joshua's feelings."

"What?" Phoebe stopped on the path beneath the branches of a big holly tree laden with red berries. "What are you talking about?"

"We all see it," Bay said, watching Joshua and Jacob move farther away from them. "He likes you. A lot. All he does is talk about you when you're not around."

Phoebe felt a flutter in her chest. He talked about her? How sweet. "He does?"

Bay pressed her lips together, which were also chapped. "And he thinks you like him." She hesitated and then went on. "Phoebe, he doesn't know your secret. I tried to tell him, but—"

"Wait," Phoebe interrupted. "What do you mean he doesn't know my secret?" She frowned, her forehead creasing. "I have no *secrets*."

"You know what I mean. He doesn't know you have a son," she answered, but not unkindly.

"My son is not a secret," Phoebe said firmly. "I've never been anything but truthful with anyone since he was born. Your mother and Benjamin knew all the details. *All* of them. I thought they told everyone in the family why I had come."

Bay chewed on her lower lip. "She only gave the particulars to me because I asked when I overheard a conversation between her and Benjamin. She didn't really think it was anyone's business. The boys, especially, I guess."

Phoebe looked away, her heart sinking. She had just assumed that Joshua knew about her son. She had assumed that because Rosemary knew, the whole family knew. No, she and Joshua hadn't talked about John-John, but she thought that was just because they hadn't reached that point in their relationship.

Would he think differently of her when he found out?

Phoebe grabbed Bay's hand. She could feel her heart pounding in her chest so hard that it was a wonder Bay couldn't hear it. What if Joshua thought less of her for what she had done? Then she couldn't be his girl. Then there could be no future with him. Then it was a mistake to tell Eli she wouldn't walk out with him. "Please believe me when I tell you I am not playing with Joshua's feelings. I promise you, I'm not." She let go of Bay's hand and strode forward.

"Phoebe, where are you going?" Bay called after her.

"To tell Joshua about my son."

Chapter Six

Phoebe hurried along the woods path, her heart pounding in her chest. How could she have made such a terrible mistake in not discussing her son with Joshua? She should have brought up her little one with him the moment she realized they might care for each other. Because if it mattered to Joshua that she had had a baby out of wedlock, then she couldn't be his girl. She could never marry him. No matter what others thought. Not even her mother.

When Phoebe and her mother had begun discussing that it was time for Phoebe to find a husband, her mother had suggested that if she could find a man willing to marry her, it wouldn't be unreasonable for him to ask that she not bring her child into the marriage. It had been done before, her mother had gently explained. Children born on the wrong side of the sheets were sometimes raised by grandparents, giving a young woman a fresh start. But Phoebe didn't want a *fresh start*. She wanted her son with her. And she wanted a husband who accepted her as the flawed, repentant woman she was.

"Joshua!" Phoebe called, walking faster, the cold breeze tugging at the hem of her dress.

"Phoebe, wait," Bay called after her. "I didn't mean to—"

"Joshua, I need to talk to you." Phoebe almost ran the last few steps to where the twin brothers stood, looking quizzically at her. "I'm sorry, Jacob," she said out of breath, "but I need to speak to Joshua. Privately." She grasped Joshua's elbow, already steering him away from his brother.

"Oh… *Ya*, sure," Jacob said, obviously feeling awkward. He exchanged glances with his brother. "Bay and I, we'll— I think I saw mistletoe this way." He trudged off the path and into the woods. "Come on, Bay," he called, waving her into the woods.

"Phoebe, what's wrong?" Joshua asked the moment Jacob and Bay were out of earshot. He looked down at her, his handsome face lined with concern.

Phoebe glanced in Bay's direction. She was cutting through the knee-high underbrush behind Jacob.

"I didn't know that you didn't know," Phoebe said, letting go of Joshua's arm when she realized she was still holding it.

He knitted his brows. "What are you talking about?"

"My secret." She shook her head, flustered. "Only he isn't a secret. I never meant for him to be a secret from you."

"Phoebe…"

He looked into her eyes, and against her will she teared up.

"Come on, let's sit," he said gently, taking her hand.

She let him lead her to a fallen tree only a few feet off the path.

He sat down on the log in a small patch of sun and patted the place beside him. "Sit and tell me what's wrong. Because I have no idea what you're talking about."

She considered staying on her feet, but she was feeling a little shaky, so she dropped down beside him. "You know what I'm talking about. My *secret*. Bay said she tried to tell you, but you wouldn't listen."

He tipped his head back, suddenly understanding. "Aah," he intoned.

"Why wouldn't you let her tell you?" she asked. She was honestly surprised by his response to his stepsister. People always wanted to know the shortcomings of others; it was in their nature. Even knowing God's teachings on the subject of gossip, it was sometimes difficult to suppress the urge to tell stories on others and listen to them.

Joshua took her mitten-covered hand in his and she let him hold it.

"I didn't let Bay tell me because I knew you would tell me anything you wanted me to know. In your own good time."

Another rush of tears came to Phoebe's eyes. She knew Joshua was a good man from the first time she met him, but now she knew that he was more than a good man. He was an exceptional one. He had the wisdom of a man twice his age. "I have a child," she whispered, looking into his face, waiting for his reaction.

"A child?" he asked. His face showed no condemnation, only puzzlement.

"A little boy. He's three." Despite her tears, she couldn't help smiling. She missed her John-John so much that it hurt. But she was so proud of him. "A beautiful little boy."

"I see." He turned her hand in his. "You were married before."

She shook her head slowly. "I was not." Her first words were almost a whisper, but as she spoke, her voice grew stronger. "John-John's father and I were betrothed to be married, but then…" She looked down at the rubber boots Rosemary had given her. They nearly matched Joshua's. She made herself look at him again. "A week before John and I were to be wed, he was killed. An accident in a silo on his father's farm."

"Oh, Phoebe," Joshua breathed. He squeezed her hand. "I am *so* sorry."

She pressed her lips together and sniffed. "Thank you," she whispered. "It was a match of our own choosing. My stepfather disapproved. A love match," she added softly.

Phoebe shifted her gaze to a cluster of pine trees in front of them, the branches heavy with weight of the snow and rain that had fallen over the last few days. She could smell the scent of the pine, clean and sweet. She watched a cardinal flit from one branch to another.

Joshua sat quietly beside her, waiting for her to find her voice again. His patience gave her the courage to go on with her story.

"I was so heartbroken," she said softly, "that I was nearly out of my mind. And then I realized I was—" It was unheard-of for an Amish woman to speak to a man not her husband of her pregnancy. But in these circumstances, she felt like she had to be completely honest with Joshua. If they had any chance to have a relationship, he had to know everything. "First, I denied my... *condition*. Then I hid it for fear my stepfather would put me out of the house."

Joshua reached into his pocket, pulled out a red handkerchief and pressed it into her hand.

"Thank you." She pulled off her mitten and wiped her eyes and then her nose. "When my mother realized I...that there was going to be a baby, we had to tell my stepfather." She hung her head wiping at her nose. "He was so angry, Joshua. Violent," she whispered.

Joshua stiffened beside her. "He hit you?" he asked, a sudden edge of anger in his voice. It was the first time she had ever heard him angry.

"Ne." She bit down hard on her lower lip, remembering that night. "He did not. But only because my mother was there, I think." She closed her eyes for a moment and took a deep breath. "He broke things. He threw them. My mother's china dishes. A chair. He dragged me out of the house in a snowstorm. Took me to our bishop." She closed her eyes and then opened them again. "It was terrible, Joshua. But I confessed what I had done, the sin I had committed. I confessed before my stepfather, my bishop and later the whole church. And God forgave." She met his gaze, her voice trembling. "It's His promise. If we confess our sins, He will be just and forgive us," she said, quoting words she had heard her preacher speak many times. "I truly believe that."

"But your stepfather didn't." It was a statement, not a question.

"He said he did, but he didn't act like it." Her voice was barely above a whisper again. The memory of that time was so difficult to recall that she felt sick to her stomach. Edom had been so cruel when her pregnancy began to show and after John-John was born. He treated her like a servant from the days of the Old Testament even though the Amish did not believe in servitude. And he treated John-John as if he were a leper. Which made her suspicious as to why he would have allowed her son to call him *vadder*.

Phoebe stared at the red handkerchief in her hands. "Say something," she said after what seemed like long moments of silence.

Joshua exhaled loudly. "I…" He exhaled with a whoosh and got to his feet. "I…I don't know what to say, Phoebe." He began to pace in front of her. "I'm angry at your stepfather and sad for you and—" He looked at her again. "I'm *so* sad for you, so sorry."

She pressed her lips together, fighting another wave of tears. "You don't…think less of me?"

"Think *less* of you?" He pulled his gloves off and tucked them in his coat pockets. Then he stood in front of her, taking her hands in his. "I think *more* of you. I cannot imagine how difficult your life has been for the last three years. I…I admire your spiritual and emotional strength." He dropped down to sit beside her again, still holding her hands. "Phoebe, I admire you. For having endured the loss of a man you loved. For having to live with a man like this stepfather of yours and still being able to find the good in this crazy world."

"You don't care that I committed the sin of adultery?" She lowered her head. "He wasn't yet my husband."

"We all sin, Phoebe."

"Not like—"

"Ne," he interrupted. "Don't do that. Don't speak against God's word. He offers us forgiveness and we have to take it. Otherwise—" He shrugged. "We're all lost, aren't we? If we can't believe in God's promises to us?"

Phoebe just sat there for a moment, feeling the warmth of Joshua's hands. Savoring it. It felt so good to feel another's touch that she considered not continuing this conversation any longer today. A part of her just wanted to go join Jacob and Bay, carrying this feeling of comfort Joshua had offered. But she knew she shouldn't, that she couldn't.

She dug deep inside herself and went on. "You said the other day that…that you wanted me to be your girl," she said. She looked up at him, feeling shy all of a sudden. "Is that something…is that something you still want?"

His mouth broadened into a grin. "Would you… would you actually consider that, Phoebe? Being my girl?" His last words were filled with excitement. "Do you…do you think you could care for me, Phoebe? Because I…I think I'm falling—"

"Don't say it," she whispered.

It seemed like a very long moment that they sat there beside each other on the log. For those few seconds, she didn't feel the chill of the wind or the little blister on her heel. The wet, fragrant forest and the faint sounds of animals scurrying about faded into the background. Nothing mattered but her and Joshua. Finally she looked away from him. "Not yet…" she told him, her voice sounding breathy in her ears. "Let's not say anything like that yet."

"Does that mean—" He stopped and started again. "Right. You're right. We need to spend time together, get to know each other better. You need time."

"Ya," she agreed. "And you need to think this over. Because, Joshua, I only want to be your girl if your intention is to marry me." The last words were hard for her to say. It seemed like a lot to ask when they had only known each other a month. When he was younger than she was and hadn't really dated yet. When she'd just told him about her son. But she didn't have time to waste playing young folks' games. Her son didn't have time. He needed to be reunited with her as soon as possible. It was only fair that Joshua know that she wasn't interested in casual dating like some young Amish men and women were.

He grabbed her hand. "I would marry you today."

"Knowing I have a child by a man who was not my husband?" she pressed, wanting to be absolutely sure they understood each other.

"Absolutely," he said firmly. "My father taught me the meaning of forgiveness when I was just a little boy."

Phoebe hadn't been entirely certain of her feelings for Joshua until that moment, but if there was any doubt in her mind, she was certain then. If she didn't already love him, she was falling in love with him. Which made no sense to her because how could she love Joshua when she had loved John? Joshua was nothing like John. John, who had been years older than she was had been blond with blue eyes, loud, brash at times. He was nothing like this gentle man who was younger than her.

"I'm sure, Phoebe," he insisted. "I have to say I was a little worried that I had… I don't know, misunderstood what I thought might be between us. Eli cornered you at the singing at Fishers' and the two of you talked forever. Then he came to the house on Thanksgiving, then again Sunday. I was afraid he was going to ask if he could court you and you were going to say yes."

She debated whether or not to tell him that Eli had already asked her. Was it fair to tell him Eli's business? But it wouldn't be fair not to tell him, and she knew he was the kind of person who would never bring it up to Eli or anyone else. "He asked to court me. On Thursday. But I said no, Joshua. Because…" She swallowed hard, wondering why it was so difficult for her to tell him how she felt about him. Maybe because it was difficult to open her heart to him when her heart had been shattered in so many pieces when John died. "I told him no because I knew I…already had feelings for you," she confessed.

"Did you tell him that?"

She looked up at him and shook her head slowly. "It didn't seem right. Not when you and I had no agreement."

"But we do now," he said firmly. "So, we can tell anyone we like now, *ya*?"

She thought for a moment, looking up into the bare branches of the oak tree over their heads. "I think we should wait a little while. Not because I don't know how I feel, but because I think you need to have some time to think on it. Because, if you marry me, you'll be agreeing to be my son's father."

"I understand that. I…I'd feel blessed to call your son mine."

She smiled at him, thinking his innocence was sweet. She knew he had no idea what it was like to be a father. But what had she known when she became a mother? What did any first-time parent know? All she had known when John-John was born was that she loved him, and the rest had fallen into place. She had the faith that it would be the same with Joshua, should this unlikely union be God's wish. "You haven't even met him," she teased.

"Doesn't matter." He squeezed her hand and then let go. "Anyway, I'm fine with that. Waiting. Just don't make me wait too long to tell anyone." He pointed at her. "Because right now, I want to shout it from the rooftop of our barn." He threw out his arms. "Phoebe Miller is my girl!"

"Shh." She grabbed his arm, afraid Jacob and Bay would hear him. Then she laughed and at the same time felt herself blushing. John's and her love had been mostly unspoken. For all of John's carefree ways, he hadn't been one to talk much of his love for her. But he *had* loved her, fiercely; she was sure of that. Who knew? Maybe these newly budding feelings she had for Joshua were possible because of John's love for her, not in spite of it. Maybe his love for her was what was making her strong enough to let herself fall in love again. His love and God's.

When she met Joshua's gaze again, he was grinning at her.

"I suppose we should go find Jacob and Bay before they start to wonder what we're up to." He rose and offered his hand to her.

Phoebe took it, not because she needed help getting up but because she wanted to feel his touch again. In truth, she was half tempted to wrap her arms around him and give him a quick hug.

He beat her to it. As she stood, he threw his arms around her. "I guess it would be too much to ask if I could have a kiss?" he said softly, looking into her eyes.

She had to take a breath to keep herself from lowering her head to his shoulder and returning the hug. "It would be, Joshua Miller," she said, trying to sound stern. "The next man I kiss will be my husband."

He let go of her, clearly not offended. "But don't the Englishers have that tradition?"

"What?" she asked.

"Something to do with kissing and mistletoe?"

She looked at him, having no idea what he was talking about. Then he pointed upward, and she lifted her gaze. High in the oak tree, directly overhead was a big ball of mistletoe.

Phoebe laughed and Joshua joined her, and somehow, in her heart, she knew that if they did wed, their home would be filled with laughter.

Joshua was just walking up toward the back door when he saw Phoebe step out onto the porch steps and throw a pan of potato skins to the chickens that were scratching around in the mud. At once they raced toward the scattered peels and began pecking at the ground. Joshua stood there watching Phoebe for a moment, taking in her beauty and imagining what it would be like to be her husband. He knew he was young to marry. He knew that's what his father would say when he and Phoebe decided to make the announcement. But he also knew that his father was a wise man, and once he talked to him he knew he would have his blessing.

The past few weeks had been beyond Joshua's expectation. He and Phoebe hadn't had much time to spend together, but every moment seemed better than the one before. He just couldn't get enough of her. She was smart and funny and kind and gentle. And truly a woman who tried to walk in her faith. When he had told Phoebe that he admired her more because of what she had gone through, he had meant it. His admiration for her grew steadily. As did his love. Of course, at Phoebe's insistence, they were never alone together. They made sure they were always within sight of someone else. And while he would have liked to have been able to spend more time with her, for the time being, he was content just to steal a few minutes with her here and there. Which had been exactly his intention when he'd walked up to the house.

"Phoebe," he called.

She looked, smiled and then waved at him as he approached.

"Do you have a minute?" he asked.

She glanced over her shoulder in the direction of the door. "I should probably get back inside. The boys are playing with Hannah's grandsons while she visits with Rosemary, but I have the potatoes to put on for supper and—"

He walked up the steps and stopped one below her.

"Five minutes. You can spare five minutes. I want you to see something down at the barn."

She balanced the pan on her hip, seeming to be trying to make up her mind.

"Come on. Get your coat. Five minutes and you'll be back. I promise."

She took a deep breath, and he watched the cloud of white as she exhaled. "Okay," she said with a grin. "But only five minutes."

She was back in just a minute, minus the potato pan, wearing a denim barn jacket that the girls all shared. "Brr, it's cold out here," she murmured as she fell into step beside him. "What do you have to show me?"

"Just wait." He looked at her and grinned.

"You're showing me something in the barn?"

"Ya," he answered, sliding his hands into his pockets, not so much because he was cold but because his hand ached to hold hers. "Something Ethan brought home from school today."

His oldest brother, Ethan was the Hickory Grove schoolmaster. Though some thought it inappropriate that a man who was thirty-two and single be the teacher, most of the families in their community thought he was the best teacher they'd had in years. He was dedicated to his students, so dedicated that he'd been known to walk several miles in the cold and snow, just to check on a boy or girl who had missed a couple of days of school. And he always had a kind ear to lend when one of the teenage boys was struggling to get along with his parents.

Joshua adored his brother Ethan, who was not only smart, but who seemed wise beyond his years. He only wished that he would step out of his shell and start dating again. His wife had been dead nearly five years now. It was time. He'd even tried a couple of times since they moved to Delaware to talk to Ethan about it, but his brother was stubborn. He wouldn't even discuss the matter. He just said he would never marry again.

"You're going to show me schoolwork?" Phoebe giggled.

"I'm not telling you." Joshua laid his hand on her arm and steered her around a mud puddle in the barnyard. "You're worse than Jesse. You'll have to wait and see."

She smiled up at him and he could feel his heart almost growing in his chest. Since their talk in the woods that day, they'd grown closer. She was so easy to be with, so kind, so much fun. The night before, after supper, Tara had made popcorn and the family had gathered in the living room to play a guessing game that had had them all laughing. Benjamin had not only been able to imitate a cow and a goose, but also a bear. Phoebe had laughed and laughed, and later she had told him that she had never known a family could live the way they lived. And the longer she stayed with Joshua's family, the more eager she said she was to retrieve John-John. They had actually talked about when would be a good time to bring him, at least for a visit. Phoebe told him she was just waiting for the right moment to bring it up with Rosemary.

"Ethan?" Joshua called as he pushed open the barn door.

Phoebe stepped in ahead of him and took a deep breath.

Joshua's father had always demanded excellent care

of their animals and their barns. The inside of the two-story barn where the horses and goats were kept was as neat as Rosemary's kitchen, and smelled of fresh hay and molasses from the tubs of grain lined up along the wall.

"You in here?" Joshua called.

"Ya," Ethan replied, his deep voice a rumble. "In the tack room."

"I brought Phoebe to see." He pointed the way for her.

She stopped in the doorway and Joshua walked up behind her, sticking his head inside. Ethan sat on an old milking stool, a bit of old flannel on his lap.

"She doing okay?" Joshua asked.

"Ya," Ethan said, moving his hand gently. "Want to see, Phoebe?" He pushed away a bit of the flannel to show a tiny white kitten.

"Oh." She sighed. "It has pink eyes."

"An albino," Ethan said, stroking the kitten.

"Rosemary won't let him bring stray students home, so he brings cats. He and Nettie are a pair. She's just the same way. Ethan brings home dogs, too, and once an iguana."

Phoebe laughed. "An iguana?"

"Ya, it's like a lizard. A big one. Rosemary refused to have it in her house. He took it to a pet shop in Dover."

She put out her hands. "Can I hold it?"

"Sure." Ethan rose from the stool and handed her the kitten, still wrapped in the flannel. "I need to change for chores, anyway." He stepped past them, halting in the door. "Just put her in the wooden box there on the floor when you go."

"Dat know you brought home another cat?" Joshua asked. "He was just saying the other morning that we're nearly overrun with them."

"Timothy's parents were going to drown it," Ethan explained. "They said it was an abomination. He smuggled it to school in his lunch box." He raised his hand and lowered it. "How could I tell him I couldn't take it?"

Joshua shook his head. "An albino cat?"

Ethan shrugged. "It's plenty healthy. I bet it will grow up to be a good mouser."

When his brother was gone, Joshua turned to watch Phoebe settle down on the milking stool. She cuddled the kitten in her arms, petting its little head with one finger. Just watching her, he could tell what a good mother she was. He could just imagine how wonderful she would be with their children, if God so blessed them with little ones. And he prayed He would.

"Know what I was thinking?"

She shook her head no, mesmerized by the kitten.

"That John-John would like her. The kitten. I thought maybe you could go fetch him for Christmas. It's only two weeks away. Rosemary might even let you keep her in your room if John-John would like that."

"Oh," she breathed. "He would love that." She looked up at him. "Even if she has to stay here in the barn. My stepfather never allowed animals in the house. We weren't even allowed to name them. No pets. Animals are just here to serve us, according to him."

Joshua slid his hands into his pockets and leaned against the doorjamb. He was feeling good today. He and Bay had gotten together after breakfast and finalized plans for the building of their greenhouse. He'd

"FAST FIVE" READER SURVEY

Your participation entitles you to:
✳ **Up to 4 FREE BOOKS and Thank-You Gifts Worth Over $20!**

Complete the survey in minutes.

Romance | Suspense

Get Up to 4 **FREE** Books

Your Thank-You Gifts include up to **4 FREE BOOKS** and **2 Mystery Gifts**. There's no obligation to purchase anything!

See inside for details.

Dear Reader,

Since you are a lover of our books, your opinions are important to us... and so is your time.

That's why we made sure your **"FAST FIVE" READER SURVEY** can be completed in just a few minutes. Your answers to the five questions will help us remain at the forefront of women's fiction.

And, as a thank-you for participating, we'd like to send you up to **4 FREE BOOKS** and **FREE THANK-YOU GIFTS!**

Try **Love Inspired® Romance Larger-Print** books featuring Christian characters facing modern-day challenges.

Try **Love Inspired® Suspense Larger-Print** novels featuring Christian characters facing challenges to their faith... and lives.

Or TRY BOTH!

Enjoy your gifts with our appreciation,

Pam Powers

To get up to
4 FREE BOOKS & THANK-YOU GIFTS:

✳ Quickly complete the "Fast Five" Reader Survey
and return the insert.

"FAST FIVE" READER SURVEY

1 Do you sometimes read a book a second or third time? ○ Yes ○ No

2 Do you often choose reading over other forms of entertainment such as television? ○ Yes ○ No

3 When you were a child, did someone regularly read aloud to you? ○ Yes ○ No

4 Do you sometimes take a book with you when you travel outside the home? ○ Yes ○ No

5 In addition to books, do you regularly read newspapers and magazines? ○ Yes ○ No

YES! Please send me my Free Rewards, consisting of **2 Free Books from each series I select** and **Free Mystery Gifts**. I understand that I am under no obligation to buy anything, as explained on the back of this card.

❏ **Love Inspired® Romance Larger-Print** (122/322 IDL GNSN)
❏ **Love Inspired® Suspense Larger-Print** (107/307 IDL GNSN)
❏ **Try Both** (122/322 & 107/307 IDL GNSY)

FIRST NAME	LAST NAME

ADDRESS

APT.#	CITY

STATE/PROV.	ZIP/POSTAL CODE

READER SERVICE—Here's how it works:

▲ If offer card is missing write to: Reader Service, P.O. Box 1341, Buffalo, NY 14240-8531 or visit www.ReaderService.com ▲

BUSINESS REPLY MAIL

FIRST-CLASS MAIL   PERMIT NO. 717   BUFFALO, NY

POSTAGE WILL BE PAID BY ADDRESSEE

READER SERVICE
PO BOX 1341
BUFFALO NY 14240-8571

NO POSTAGE
NECESSARY
IF MAILED
IN THE
UNITED STATES

talked briefly with his father about the idea because now that marriage was in his future, he wanted to know he had a plan with how to support his family. And the greenhouse and shop he and Bay had in mind would certainly do that in good time. Of course he hadn't mentioned his intention to marry Phoebe yet. Even though he had wanted to so many times in the past few weeks. He wouldn't do so until he and Phoebe agreed it was time.

"She's so sweet," Phoebe said, lifting the kitten to her cheek. "Thank you for showing me." She stood. "Now I need to get back to check on the boys, but thank you."

For a moment the two of them just stood there, looking into each other's eyes. And even though Joshua ached to wrap his arms around her, he knew he could wait. Because Phoebe was worth the wait, he was just sure of it.

Chapter Seven

Phoebe laughed as James lurched toward a rabbit cutting across the driveway in front of them. "I don't think you're going to catch him, not today," she told him, taking his hand, which was covered by a flannel mitten. They were walking down to the mailbox at the end of the long driveway, but the trip was taking far longer than she had anticipated. Like her son, James had to stop after every couple of steps to pick up a leaf or a rock off the ground or, in this case, try to reach for something he would never catch.

"Come on," she encouraged, trying to steer him forward. "Let's go this way." The moment she let go of his hand, though, he veered off again. This time toward the door of the harness shop.

"*Ne*, we're going to the mailbox, remember?" she told him, reaching for his hand.

James made a beeline for the door, moving as fast as his chubby little legs would carry him. "Dat!" he cried. Or something close to it.

Phoebe sighed. James had been restless all morning.

Josiah had a runny nose and wasn't feeling well. He'd been feeling so poorly that Rosemary had decided to put him down for an early nap. And like most twins Phoebe had known, James was a little lost without his sibling. That was the reason she had decided to take him for a walk, to get his mind off missing his brother. And someone needed to fetch the mail anyway because Rosemary was eagerly awaiting her latest copy of the Amish newspaper, the *Budget*. She had expected it the day before and had been quite perturbed it was late again. The paper was useful to Amish families because it included pages of advertisements for items they couldn't make easily at home, like men's hats and certain tools. More importantly, it was full of the news of Amish communities all over the United States and Canada. By way of the *Budget*, Rosemary could keep up with births and deaths and visits in their old town in New York, as well as friends and relatives in other states.

James toddled toward the shop door as his knit cap slid down over his eyes. He was dressed just like the other men in the household, in a denim coat, denim pants with suspenders and rubber boots. Chuckling, Phoebe leaned over him and adjusted his hat. "How can you see anything, you silly goose?" she asked him.

He responded with something she couldn't understand. All she caught was her name. He and Josiah both called her Fifi.

"All right," she told James. "We'll go find your *dat*, but we're only staying a minute. Your *mam* will be wanting to know where you've gotten to if you're gone too long. I would think Josiah will be up by the time we get back."

Phoebe reached over his head and pushed on the door. As it opened, a little bell jingled over her head.

James spotted his big sister behind the counter and immediately toddled in her direction.

Bay glanced up as she opened the cash register to make change for a customer. "Hi ya, Phoebe. Josh isn't here if you're looking for him," she called, counting out the dollar bills as she removed them from the drawer.

"*Ne*, we weren't." Phoebe closed the door behind her, wondering if he had said anything to Bay about the agreement between them to keep their relationship to themselves at least for a little while longer. She doubted it. Did that mean Bay had figured it out? Because if so, it wouldn't be long before everyone else in the household knew. Which made Phoebe think maybe Joshua was right, maybe it was time to sit down with Benjamin and Rosemary and discuss the matter.

Shifting her thoughts, Phoebe asked, "New wreath?" pointing to the door. The previous one had had a big red bow on it; this one was green gingham.

"*Ya.*" Bay handed the customer at the counter his change and closed the cash register drawer. She smiled up at him. "Have a good day. Merry Christmas."

"Merry Christmas," the man in a Clark's Feed baseball cap and sheepskin coat responded, taking his bag with him.

Phoebe nodded as he walked by but avoided eye contact. Bay and her sisters were so good at dealing with Englisher men. They were used to them, she supposed, what with the harness shop and having a table of items to sell during the warmer months at Spence's Bazaar. Growing up, Phoebe hadn't gotten off the farm often and when she did, she mostly interacted with other Amish women.

"Bay-Bay," James said excitedly, throwing his arms out to his sister.

Bay leaned over the counter, lifted James up and plopped him down on top of it. "A lady came yesterday and wanted to buy the one with the red bow right off the door," she said to Phoebe as she tugged her brother's cap off his head and ruffled his rusty-colored hair. "Offered an extra five dollars."

"Did you take it?" Phoebe asked.

The bell over the door rang again as the man left the shop, and she and Bay and the little one were alone.

"Ne." Bay handed James a little paper bag to play with. "I have plenty of wreaths that size in the back, pine and spruce. I just grabbed another one and put a bow on it. Nettie made the gingham bow from scraps she found in Mam's sewing room."

"I can't believe you've sold so many wreaths," Phoebe commented. "Close to fifty already, Joshua told me." She studied a shelf of jars of fruit preserves for sale, the lids covered with pretty squares of fabric.

Not only did the harness shop repair leather works and sell all sorts of bridles and harnesses and such, but they also sold assorted items for animal care and the household. And now they were selling foodstuffs: baked goods, jams and jellies, pickles and fresh eggs. Joshua had told her that Bay was behind the idea, and since the addition of such things the whole business had been booming. Men came in for harness or leather repairs, but female customers were beginning to stop by, too, just to see what the Stutzman women were selling now.

"I thought twenty dollars was too much for a wreath to begin with," Bay went on. "But an Englisher lady came in this morning and bought three. She said I was the cheapest around."

"And the nicest, I'm sure," Phoebe told her, straightening a jar of strawberry jam so that the label was front and center. "Selling many of the preserves?"

"So many that I may have to accept a couple of cases off Eunice." She rolled. "And then she'll likely be telling everyone that I couldn't sell the ones we made."

Phoebe chuckled. "I don't think she means things the way they sometimes sound. She seems like she has a good heart. She just speaks before she thinks."

"*Ya*, you're probably right. Mam says the same. But…" Bay shrugged and then lifted James into her arms. "You want to go see your *dat*?" she asked him, looking into his sweet face. He had a bright circle of red on each cheek. "I hear your *dat*'s voice, I do. He must be back from Dover."

"I didn't mean to bother you." Phoebe pushed her hands into the pockets of her denim barn coat. She'd removed her mittens when they came inside, but now she was chilly. "We were headed to the mailbox, but James insisted we come inside. Josiah is napping."

"Ah." Bay bounced James on her hip, looking down at him. "And you're missing your *bruder*, *ya*?" James smiled.

"I think so," Phoebe answered for him.

Bay glanced at her. "You want to go to the mailbox and come back for him? I'll take him to see Benjamin. Be a lot faster without him," she said, already headed for the door that led to the rear of the shop. There, Joshua and his brothers and Ginger made repairs to the leather goods that were dropped off by customers.

"True enough." Phoebe tightened her blue wool scarf under her chin. "I can stop for him on my way back to the house. If you don't mind, of course. I know you have the cash register to mind."

Bay halted in the doorway and turned back to her. "I'll hear if anyone comes in. That's why we put the bell over the door."

Phoebe smiled. *"Danke."* Then, buttoning the top of her coat and pulling her mittens out of her pocket, she stepped back out into the cold. Head down, she started for the end of the lane and the mailbox.

Phoebe had offered to walk down and check it for Rosemary, but her intention was at least partially selfish. She hadn't heard from her mother in two weeks, despite having sent her three letters, and she was hoping for news from her today. Phoebe kept telling herself it was just that her mother was busy with the little ones, a busy house to run and a demanding husband. But she still worried. The last she had heard from her, John-John was calling Edom *vadder.*

Trying not to fret, Phoebe followed the driveway the last quarter of a mile to the road. On her way, she had to get out of the lane twice for customers headed to the harness shop: first a buggy, then a red pickup truck. When she reached the big black mailbox fastened to a salt-treated post, she eagerly opened it. Sure enough, Rosemary's newspaper was there, as well as several circulars advertising sales at stores in town. Wrapped in the circulars was a phone bill, an invitation for a credit card for Ben Miller and, at last, a small white envelope with her mother's neat handwriting across the front.

Phoebe's first impulse was to rip open the letter right there, but the sun had disappeared behind the clouds and the wind had picked up. Suddenly she was chilled. So instead of standing there on the road and reading it, she hurried back to the harness shop. Once inside the door, with no sign of Bay or James, she laid the other mail on a metal shelf that displayed an assortment of flea, tick and mange products and ripped open the envelope.

The moment she unfolded the thin piece of writing paper, she knew something was wrong. The letter was short. No news of the house or the family, just three sentences that could not possibly have come from her mother. Except that she knew they did because it was her mother's handwriting, neat and dark, written with a blue pen. Her mother always wrote in blue pen.

Daughter,
After much prayer and contemplation, your step-father has made the decision to adopt John. Paperwork from the state requiring your signature will be mailed to you in Hickory Grove. We hope you are well of body and soul.
Your mother

Phoebe's chest tightened and her breath caught in her throat, and for a moment she felt as if she wasn't getting any air. She read the letter again and then a third time, certain she had misread it. But she hadn't. *Your stepfather has made the decision to adopt John.* The words cut her so deeply that she felt her heart might be bleeding. "No," she whispered. "You can't do that." She crumpled the letter in her hand. "He can't do that."

At that moment, Bay walked into the shop from the back. "Benjamin took James back up to the house. They decided they needed hot chocolate."

Phoebe nodded slowly, only half hearing what she was saying. She just couldn't believe Edom would try to take her son away from her. She couldn't believe he thought he had that right.

"Are you okay?" Bay asked, staring at her.

For a moment, Phoebe couldn't find her voice. She didn't know what to do. There was no way to call her mother to ask what the letter meant. How could Edom adopt John? Surely he had no right to do that. And even if he did think he had that right, what had ever given him, or her mother for that matter, the idea that she would even agree to such a thing? But even if she could call her mother, Phoebe knew her mother would side with her husband. She had a feeling it was Edom who had dictated the letter. Her mother would never have used the words *requiring your signature.* Her mother had been an orphan, raised by neighbors. She had only attended school until she was ten before the family began keeping her at home so she could work on their dairy farm.

"Phoebe?" Bay said, walking around the counter.

Phoebe looked up at her. She needed Joshua. He would know what to do. He would know how to keep her stepfather from taking her son. "Do…do you know where Joshua is?" she asked, her voice sounding like someone else's.

"In the smokehouse," Bay answered, concern in her voice. "Tidying up. Phoebe—"

Phoebe turned around stiffly and opened the door. The little bell rang over her head, but she barely heard it. All she could think of was putting one foot in front of the other. She had to find Joshua because she couldn't let Edom take her son. She *wouldn't* let him.

Phoebe walked back out into the cold, closing the door behind her.

A moment later, she heard it open.

"Phoebe!" Bay called after her. "You forgot the mail!"

But Phoebe didn't turn back because she had to find Joshua. She had to save her son.

The smokehouse was Phoebe's favorite outbuilding on the Miller farm. Maybe it was because her family had never had one, or maybe it was because it was another representation of the abundance here in Hickory Grove. Growing up, she remembered often going to bed hungry, not just for physical sustenance, but emotional, as well. Benjamin and Rosemary not only fed their children's bodies, but also their souls.

One foot in the door, Phoebe was overcome by the rich smells of smoked shad, salted and sugar-cured hams, and, of course, the smoked hams that hung in rows from the dark beams overhead. Feeding a large family necessitated forethought and planning. And despite the two propane-powered freezers in Benjamin and Rosemary's cellar, the smokehouse provided a good deal of the meat served on the table year-round.

"Joshua?" she called, her eyes adjusting to the dim

light that seeped through tiny windows high on two walls and covered in brown paper to protect the meats from the sunlight.

"Hey, Phoebe. Right here."

She spotted him standing on a stool.

He stretched his arm to remove a cord that held up a hefty side of smoked bacon. "It's nice to see you. I wasn't expecting—" When he made eye contact with her, he went quiet. "What's wrong?" he asked, coming down off the stool, the side of bacon dangling from his hand on a thick cord.

Phoebe just stood there, trying not to cry but not doing a good job of it. The letter from her mother was crumpled in her cold hand. "I'm sorry," she whispered, embarrassed by her tears. "I didn't know what to do... who to come to."

He set the bacon down on a makeshift table built from plywood and two sawhorses. "What is it?"

She pressed her lips together. "My son," was all she could manage.

His handsome face immediately washed with concern. "Is John-John all right?"

"Yes, fine. Not hurt or sick. But—" Her hand shaking, she handed him the letter.

Joshua took it from her hand. He was wearing a plain gray Englisher sweatshirt that had a hood, and no hat. She could see it stuffed in the front pocket. Rosemary had cut all of the men's hair the previous night. He looked younger than twenty-three with the boyish haircut and his face shaved cleanly. But she didn't see him as a boy; if she'd had any question as to whether he was mature enough to take on the responsibilities of a husband and father, the last two weeks had dispelled that. The better she got to know him, the more she realized he was actually quite mature for a single man his age.

"The letter is from my mother," she explained.

"You want me to read it?"

She nodded, not trusting she could tell him the contents without sobbing on his shoulder. Because right now, she desperately wanted to feel his strong arms around her.

He smoothed out the letter and began to read.

Phoebe hugged herself, watching him.

It only took a moment before he looked up at her. "He can't do this, Phoebe. I don't care what your mother says. He can't legally take your son without your permission. Not if you don't sign those papers."

She shook her head. "Of course I'm not signing any papers. I don't want John-John there with that man anymore." She sniffed. She was so cold that her nose was running.

He pulled a handkerchief from his pocket and handed it to her.

She blew her nose, wiped it and went on. "What if Edom were to send John-John off to relatives in another state? How would I ever find him?" She bit down on her lower lip. "My son needs to be here with me." She looked up at Joshua again. "I just don't know how to get him back."

"That's easy enough." He grabbed her hand and led her toward the open door, his stride long and determined. "We'll go get him."

Joshua stood at his father's workbench, watching him tack black fabric to a buggy seat with a heavy-duty stapler. A kerosene lamp hung above his head, casting bright yellow light across the small workshop in the rear of the dairy barn they had converted to the harness shop. Joshua was constantly amazed by his father's ability to build or fix anything. Even though Benjamin's trade was in leather works, he'd always wanted to build buggies, like his grandfather. Now, two years after moving from New York to Delaware, he'd decided to dabble in the dying trade. A buggy maker had to be a welder, an upholsterer, a carpenter, mechanic and painter all rolled into one.

"Did you speak to Rosemary about this?" Joshua's father asked.

"I came to you first."

He was clearly deep in thought. "I don't know, Joshua. It's a grave business, interfering with a man's family."

"I know, Dat," Joshua responded. "But I don't think Phoebe's fear is unfounded. I have the letter here, if you'd like to read it." He reached into the pouch pocket of his sweatshirt to remove the letter from Phoebe's mother. A hoodie wasn't exactly approved clothing for men in their church district, but their bishop accepted practicality and said nothing as long as the sweatshirts remained confined to the home and barn.

Benjamin glanced up at his son, who was taller than he was. "I don't need to read it. I'll take your word on it." He was quiet for a moment. He added several more staples to the underside of the seat, then flipped it over to check his work. The black fabric was pleated and tacked down perfectly around the corner he'd just finished. "I'm uneasy with the idea of you entering this man's house and taking his grandchild—"

"Phoebe's son," Joshua corrected, trying to temper his anger. He just couldn't believe Edom would do such a thing as to try to take a child from his mother. He'd had an idea Edom wasn't a good man, but this went beyond his understanding. "John is Phoebe's son but technically not Edom Wickey's grandson. Edom isn't Phoebe's father, but rather her stepfather."

Benjamin eyed his son. "You're talking about going there and back in the same day?"

"Ya." Joshua slid his hands into his pants pockets. "I've already talked with Shorty Davies. He can take us up and back in his van. He says it will be a long day, but he used to be a truck driver before he retired. Says he's used to long days." The sixty-five-year-old was their neighbor. He'd told Joshua that he hadn't taken well to retirement and that was why he spent his days as a hired driver for the Amish in the area. "And Bay says she'll go with us," Joshua added.

"So you won't give Eunice Gruber reason to talk. A single man and a single woman, unescorted. Good thinking." Benjamin flipped the seat back over and picked up the stapler. "Well…if you think this is best, you have my blessing. I like Phoebe. She's good to Rosemary and the littles love her to bits. Her past is no reason for her stepfather to treat her this way. Or the boy. A child that age belongs with his mother."

"It's settled." Joshua tapped the edge of the workbench with his knuckles. "We'll go tomorrow and bring the little one home."

"Ya, but any trouble—" Benjamin met his son's gaze "—and you use Shorty's cell phone and you call me." He stroked his rusty-colored beard, which was begin-

ning to gray. "And I'll come up there myself and get the boy."

Joshua grinned. "*Danke*, Dat." He turned to go, but his father called his name. *"Ya?"* he said, looking back.

"I know some see pride in their children as *hockmut*. But I don't see it that way." Benjamin turned on the wooden stool he sat perched on and removed the glasses he wore for doing close work. "I'm proud of you, *sohn*. That you would take up for Phoebe when she has no man to do it for her."

Embarrassed by his father's praise, Joshua nodded, not making eye contact with him. "We leave at five thirty tomorrow morning. I'll use Shorty's phone to call you at the shop and let you know once we have the boy and we're safely on our way home."

Joshua walked out of his father's workshop and hurried through the dark barn, eager to tell Phoebe the arrangements were made.

He was nervous to come face-to-face with Edom. After all the things Phoebe had told him, he didn't much like the man. But he was also excited to bring Phoebe's son home, because if everything worked out the way he was praying it would, he'd be bringing home his own son, too.

Chapter Eight

Phoebe sat on the middle seat of the van beside Bay, twisting her fingers together in her lap. She stared out the window. There had been a heavy snow the evening before in northwestern Pennsylvania, so heavy that she had feared the driver Joshua had hired would cancel their trip. But as promised, he had shown up early that morning at the Miller house to take them to New Wilmington to fetch John-John. Rosemary and Benjamin had seen them off with egg and scrapple sandwiches and two large thermoses of hot coffee for breakfast, which was enough for Phoebe, Bay, Josh and their driver. There were also sandwiches and cold salads for lunch. The plan was to stop for dinner somewhere on the turnpike, once they were on their way home.

They passed the road sign welcoming them to New Wilmington and a heaviness settled in Phoebe's stomach. It wasn't that she wasn't excited to see her little boy, to feel him in her arms again, because she was. But she was dreading the confrontation with Edom, a confrontation she knew would take place. There was no way he would simply allow Phoebe to walk out of the house with her son. And she was worried about Joshua's safety. What if Joshua defended her and Edom became violent? She knew from experience that her mother wouldn't intervene. Elsie Wickey was either unwilling or unable. Phoebe wasn't sure which. Her only hope was that Joshua would keep a cool head even if her stepfather did not.

Phoebe couldn't imagine what this trip had cost Joshua. She'd tried to find out the last time they had stopped to use the restroom. He'd bought everyone, including the driver, a hot chocolate with fluffy marshmallows at Starbucks. He'd also bought them crunchy gingerbread cookies called biscotti. And refused to let her pay for her own drink or tell her how much it had cost him to hire a driver and van for the day. He kept telling her not to worry about it, but she had promised she would pay him back. She wasn't even sure how she would do it. She had little money of her own. But she and Bay had been talking about making wreaths for other seasons, and she had suggested ones made from grapevines that could be decorated in various ways. An hour later they had a plan to make not just grapevine wreaths, but swags to go over doors and such, and Bay had offered to pay her to make them. The idea was to sell them in the greenhouse shop Bay and Joshua hoped to have built by spring.

"Phoebe, you okay?" Joshua asked gently from the front passenger seat of Shorty's minivan.

Phoebe glanced at Bay, who was knitting while staring out the window, tapping her foot to Christian music playing on the radio. Technically, they weren't supposed to listen to radios, but Joshua had assured them that because it was Shorty's vehicle and he had chosen Christian music, it was okay. Apparently, Bay loved music like this, because she was so focused on the tunes that she wasn't paying any attention to Phoebe and Joshua.

"I'm all right," Phoebe said, keeping her voice down. "Just nervous."

"No need to be," he insisted. He reached out as if he was going to take her hand and then pulled back, she suspected for fear Bay might see him. "I'll be right there with you."

Phoebe closed her eyes, saying a prayer. She thanked God for Joshua and asked Him to deliver her son safely into her hands. "You don't know Edom," she said when she opened her eyes again. "He's going to be very angry."

"He'll have to deal with that anger himself, Phoebe. Because that's not our problem." His tone sounded confident and strongly masculine. "You're doing nothing wrong."

She glanced out the window again and saw her own reflection in the glass. She had dressed carefully in the same clothing she'd been wearing when she had gotten on the bus almost two months ago to go to Hickory Grove. She wore her black dress, black stockings, black shoes, black dress bonnet over her prayer *kapp* and the heavy black wool coat that had been a hand-me-down from years ago. Clothes that didn't seem like they belonged to her anymore. Not when she had a blue dress and a green one and a new cloak Rosemary had sewn for her.

"I just want this to be over," she said softly.

"And it will be." He met her gaze, his dark brown eyes warm with caring. He was dressed in his Sunday clothes of all black, and a black hat and coat. "We'll be in and out of there in a couple of minutes. You get your son and bring him back to the van, where Bay, Shorty and I will wait. Then you go back in for anything you want, anything of yours or John-John's."

"I don't want anything of Edom's," she said, shaking her head adamantly.

Joshua opened his arms wide. "Then this will be even quicker. Before you know it, we'll be on the road heading south. And you'll have your son, and no one will separate the two of you again." He hesitated. "Okay?" he asked gently.

She couldn't resist the faintest smile. His optimism was contagious. "Okay," she responded.

Ten minutes later, they pulled into her stepfather's barnyard, which in no way resembled Joshua's father's place. While the Miller farm was neat and orderly, Edom Wickey's place was not so well cared for. The dilapidated farmhouse was a two-story frame structure with tall brick chimneys at either end. Behind and to the sides loomed several barns, sheds and outbuildings, all missing shingles and in need of repair. A derelict windmill, missing more than half of its blades, leaned precariously to one side. None of the recent snow had been cleared, and a dog barked hungrily from atop the doghouse it was chained to. The two driving horses in the pasture looked thin and cold and were without blankets.

Phoebe saw the state of unkempt property register on Joshua's face, but he said nothing.

"Pull up there please, Shorty," she instructed, pointing to the back porch.

The moment the van rolled to a stop, Joshua was out of the van. He opened the sliding door and offered his hand to Phoebe, who was already out of her seat belt.

"We'll be back in a couple of minutes," Joshua said.

"I'll move the car seat up," Bay offered, setting down her knitting. "John-John will want to sit with his mother."

"We can sit in the back." Phoebe stepped down out of the van and into the snow without Joshua's aid. "I don't mind," she told Bay.

"Nonsense. I like the back. I might even stretch out and take a nap on the way home."

Phoebe heard the screen door of the back porch open and then close. She turned, steeling herself to see Edom. To her relief, it wasn't him, but her mother.

"Phoebe!"

Elsie Wickey was a tall, thin, sallow-faced woman with a narrow beak of a nose, a wide mouth and very little chin. But to Phoebe, she had always been beautiful. "Mam," Phoebe croaked, running through the snow and up the rickety porch steps to throw her arms around her mother's bony shoulders.

"What are you doing here?" Phoebe's mother asked, hugging her daughter tightly. "You shouldn't have come."

Phoebe drew back, wiping a tear from her cheek. "I had to come back, Mam. For John-John."

Her mother's thin mouth twitched. She looked older to Phoebe than she had when she'd left. And she appeared tired and sickly. Her nose was running and cheeks chafed. "Edom won't allow it."

"I'm sorry, Elsie, but that's not up to him." Joshua took the porch steps two at a time. "I'm Joshua Miller, Rosemary's stepson. Benjamin's son."

Phoebe turned to Joshua. "Joshua and Rosemary's daughter Bay brought me here to fetch John-John. I'm taking him, Mam. Back to Hickory Grove."

Her mother hesitated, then grasped her daughter's forearm. "Hurry then. Edom's expected back anytime." She held open the back door that was sagging on its ill-fitting hinges. "John-John's in the kitchen with the girls."

Phoebe turned to Joshua, embarrassed by the condition of the house. Everywhere paint was peeling, the clapboard siding was rotting, and the porch posts were leaning, the sagging rails, on their last legs. "Wait here," she instructed. "I'll be just a moment."

He didn't seem happy with her request. "Are you sure?"

Phoebe nodded quickly and then leaned forward to whisper to him. "Watch for him. Call me if he comes up the lane. I want to see my sisters and brothers. Just to be sure they're all right."

The look on Joshua's face suggested he was debating whether or not to do as she asked, but after a moment he nodded sharply. "Hurry. It would be best if we could be out of here before he returns."

Phoebe reached out and gave his bare hand a squeeze, then followed her mother into the house. Phoebe didn't take off her shoes even though she was tracking snow into the house. She didn't intend to stay long enough to need to remove her shoes. They passed through the dark mudroom, where there were piles of laundry on the floor, and into the kitchen. The low-ceilinged room was lit by kerosene lanterns hanging from the exposed, smoke-stained beams overhead. It was nearly as cold inside as it was out. She glanced at the wood stove. "Mam, have you no wood?"

"We have wood," she murmured. "But Edom has taken to doling it out. I have to save it for cooking."

The moment they entered the kitchen, her four step-sisters and youngest stepbrother began calling her name, squealing with excitement and all talking at once, obviously happy to see her.

"Schweschder!"

"Schweschder!"

"Phoebe!" Seventeen-year-old Ephrath squealed and ran across the kitchen to throw her arms around her stepsister's shoulders.

Phoebe hugged her tightly. "Ephrath. It's so good to see you."

"Did Mam tell you?" she whispered. "I'm to be married. Next month."

"Married?" Phoebe drew back, staring at her. "But you're so young to marry."

"I'm going to get out of here," her younger sister whispered in Phoebe's ear. "His name is Noah and he lives in Ohio." She clasped her red, chapped hands together excitedly. "I'm moving to Ohio!"

Phoebe met her gaze. "This is what you want?"

Ephrath nodded. "I've not yet met him, but—"

"Not met him?" Phoebe interrupted, trying to keep

her shock from her voice. She turned to her mother. "You're marrying her off to—"

"*Ne, ne.* I *want* to marry Noah," Ephrath insisted. "We've been writing." Her thin cheeks grew rosy. "He's very kind. He's an apprentice to a mason. He says he can build our house himself come spring."

Phoebe sighed, letting her arms fall to her sides. She and Rosemary had had a talk the night before. Phoebe had expressed her feelings of guilt that she and John-John were escaping life with Edom, but her mother and stepsiblings were not. Rosemary had insisted that she had to concentrate on her son and herself and have faith that God would protect those she loved.

"Mam will give you my address in Hickory Grove, then," Phoebe told her stepsister. She grasped her hands. "Write to me once you're married."

Ephrath bounced up and down on her toes. "Of course."

Phoebe looked around the cold, dim kitchen. Though it was spotlessly clean, it was as in need of repair as the exterior of the house and the outbuildings. Several panes in the window above the sink were covered in cardboard, the glass broken for many years. The paint on the walls was peeling, and the beams overhead were black with smoke. "Where's John-John?" she breathed, suddenly just wanting to grab him and run from the house.

"He was here a second ago. John-John? Where are you?" Ephrath called in Pennsylvania *Deutsch.*

"John-John?" Phoebe was suddenly near to tears. "It's your *mam*. Where are you?"

And then she spotted him, peering out from under the wobbly kitchen table.

"Mammi?" he said in a tiny voice.

"Oh, John-John." Phoebe crouched down, opening her arms to him.

For a moment he hesitated, looking at her with solemn eyes that reflected his father's. Then his rosebud mouth turned up in a smile and he crawled out from under the table on all fours.

"Oh, John-John," Phoebe breathed, pulling her son into her arms. She closed her eyes, breathing deeply. He smelled as if he needed a good wash in the tub with a bar of soap, but he also had that scent of the child born of her own body that she would never forget. "Mam's come to take you home," she whispered in his ear. "Home to our new house."

The little boy clung to her. "Mammi," he kept saying. "Mammi."

Phoebe hugged him for another moment and then stood, lifting him into her arms. She wiped at her eyes as she turned to her mother. As she spoke, she moved from one sister to the next and then to her little brother, hugging them all. "His coat and hat, *mam*? We should go now."

"Phoebe?" Joshua called through the screen door. His voice sounded deeper and more sober than she had ever heard before. "There's a rig coming up the lane."

"It's Edom!" Phoebe's mother cried, bringing her hands to her head, which was covered in an old scarf. "Phoebe, you have to hurry."

One of Phoebe's little sisters began to cry, and Phoebe rushed out of the kitchen carrying John-John. "I'm coming!" she called. "Where's his coat? It's bitter out."

"He shares one with Saul," Phoebe's mother said. She grabbed an old quilt from a pile of dirty clothes on the laundry room floor.

Unlike most Amish homes, they did not have modern appliances running off a generator or propane. Her mother still washed clothes in an old-fashioned ringer washer and hung everything to dry. In the winter, when clothes would only freeze on the line, they hung them in the attic. And because washing was so time-consuming, her mother sometimes fell behind on washing day, causing clothes to pile up.

"Wrap him up in this," her mother told her, putting it around John-John's shoulders.

"Not your *grossmama*'s quilt," Phoebe protested. "It's the only thing you have left of hers."

"Go," her mother insisted, pushing her toward the back door, where Joshua waited for them.

"Get into the van," Joshua instructed, waving her through the door. Though his face was lined with concern, his tone was gentle. "*Now*, Phoebe. I'll handle this."

"Joshua." Phoebe gazed up into his dark eyes. "This isn't your fight."

"It became mine when I met you," he whispered in her ear as she went by.

"Will you be all right, Mammi?" Phoebe asked over her shoulder as she hurried across the porch, wobbly with its soft spots where it had rotted through.

"Go, *dochtah*. Don't worry about me," her mother fretted. "He always comes to his senses once he calms down."

Phoebe didn't know that she agreed with her, but

what she did know was that her first responsibility was to the safety of her child, even above her mother. Most certainly above herself.

As Phoebe hurried down the steps, clutching John-John to her, covered by the quilt, the sliding door to the van flew open and Bay stood there, her arms out. "Pass him to me," she murmured.

"I don't know if he'll come to you."

"Here we go, little one," Bay cooed in Pennsylvania *Deutsch*. She reached for him.

It was difficult for Phoebe to let go of her son, but Edom had just pulled up in his buggy. He had angled it so that Shorty couldn't pull away in the van without risking startling or harming the old driving horse.

"Could you pull up a few feet?" Joshua hollered to Edom, waving at him. "We're on our way out."

"I will not!" Edom shouted hostilely, coming down out of the buggy. "Who are you? What are you doing here?"

Phoebe handed John to Bay, kissing the top of his head as she passed him off. "Go with Bay," she whispered. "Mammi is coming in just a minute." Covering his head with the quilt as if her great-grandmother's stitching could somehow protect her son, she told Bay, "Put him into his car seat. Buckle him in. Do you know how to do it?"

Shorty owned the car seat for his Amish customers because it was Englisher law that children had to be in car seats. Phoebe had never used one.

"We've used them for James and Josiah," Bay assured her.

Bay closed the sliding door and Phoebe walked around to the front of the van.

"Phoebe, please get in the van," Joshua said, holding his hand out to stop her.

"I asked you what you were—" Edom halted in the middle of his sentence when he saw Phoebe. "You," he said in Pennsylvania *Deutsch*. "You weren't supposed to come back here! Not ever."

"I came back for John-John," she said. Her voice was strong despite the fact that she was shaking inside.

"You're not taking him!" her stepfather declared, striding toward the front of the van where Phoebe and Joshua stood.

Edom Wickey was a surprisingly handsome man with a full head of dark hair and no gray in his beard yet. He was dressed impeccably in Sunday clothes, his wool pants and coat pressed, his white shirt pristine. He wore an expensive wide-brimmed wool hat on his head and a black cashmere scarf around his neck. Phoebe knew it was cashmere because she had heard her mother and Edom arguing over the purchase the winter before when she had tried to tell him that they could have bought wool scarves for everyone in the family for what he had spent. The argument, like all of them, ended with Edom shouting and her mother crying and then retreating.

Edom drew so close to Phoebe that she had to steel herself to keep from stepping back. It was one of his methods of intimidating people. He always stood too close and spoke too loudly.

"He's my son," Phoebe said softly. "You have no legal right to him."

"Legal right!" Edom exploded, sending spittle into the air. "I am your guardian, girl! I have a right to do whatever I want with you or your spawn!"

"Edom, please!" Phoebe's mother came running down the porch steps, wearing no coat and only socks on her feet. "Let them go."

"Get in the house, woman!" Edom barked. "I'll deal with you later."

"Edom," Joshua said, his voice taking on a steely tone. "Move your rig. We're leaving."

"You can take her!" he spit, pointing an accusing finger at Phoebe. "But not the boy!"

Joshua turned to Phoebe. "Get in the van. Tell Shorty to start it up." He leaned close to her and whispered in her ear, "I give you the signal, you tell Shorty to back up, pull around and head out."

Phoebe grabbed Joshua's arm, gazing into his eyes.

"You can pick me up at the end of the lane." He winked at her. "I'm sure I can run faster than he can in those fancy clothes."

Had the circumstances been any different, Phoebe might have laughed.

"Go on." Joshua gave her a nudge.

"Hand over the boy and you can be on your way," Edom ordered, slapping the side of the van with his gloved hand.

Phoebe's mother caught her husband's arm. "Let them go, Edom. They're nothing but trouble, the both of them. You said so yourself."

"Legally, Edom," Joshua said, "you can't keep this boy and you know it."

"Are you threatening me with Englisher laws?" Edom sputtered. "Who are you, boy?"

"I'm Benjamin Miller's son, Joshua Miller of Miller's Harness in Hickory Grove, Delaware."

"What business of this is yours?"

Phoebe's mother spoke up with a trembling voice. "I think what my husband is asking is what your intention is with my daughter."

"My intention?" Joshua leaned so close to Edom that their noses were practically touching. "My *intention* is to marry Phoebe. Which means, according to *our* ways, John will soon be my son." Not waiting for a reply, Joshua put his hand on Phoebe's shoulder and gently pushed her in the direction of the van.

Edom still stood there, seeming shocked that someone would stand up to him.

Joshua opened the van door for Phoebe. "You best move your rig, Edom," he called.

Elsie left her husband's side, hurrying toward the van door. "Take care, daughter. Know that I loved you the best I could." Tears ran down her flushed, thin face. "And John-John. Tell him when he's older that his *grossmami* loves him."

Tears in her eyes, Phoebe turned and threw her arms around her mother. "Try to write to me."

"*Ya,*" her mother responded. Although they both knew Edom would never allow any correspondence between them again. "Be happy, daughter. He's a good man, your Joshua."

Phoebe hugged her mother again. "*Ya,* he is," she whispered. "I think he loves me, Mam."

"And you?" she whispered in her daughter's ear. "Do you love him?"

Phoebe was so overcome with emotion, with thankfulness for Joshua's help, that at the moment she didn't even know how to answer. Because what was love? There was the romantic love, of course, the kind that made your stomach flutter. But there was also the kind of love a woman felt for a man who risked his own well-being to rescue a woman's child. She certainly felt that love for him. She also suspected she loved him romantically. But everything was in such turmoil. How could she know for sure? But when she looked in her mother's eyes, she knew what her answer had to be. At least to leave her mother content in knowing she and John-John would be safe and cared for.

Phoebe forced a smile, peering into her mother's face, knowing it might be the last time she ever saw her stepsiblings again. "I think I'm falling in love with him, Mam."

Elsie hugged her daughter one last time and then pushed her none too gently. "Go."

Joshua was right behind Phoebe as she got into the van.

"Fine!" Edom shouted. "Take her! Take them both! But don't ever bring them back here. A jezebel like her—"

Joshua jumped into the van and slammed the sliding door shut, muffling Edom's words until they were unintelligible. He leaned between the two front seats. "Can you get around him?" he asked the driver.

"Sure can. Just have to back up a little," Shorty told him.

Joshua turned to Phoebe. "Get your seat belt on." He

slid into the front passenger seat as Shorty threw the van into Reverse. "Bay?" he called.

"All buckled up. John-John, too," she called from the back.

Tears rolling down her cheeks, Phoebe reached for her son's chubby hand. His eyes were round with fear and confusion, but he wasn't making a peep.

"What a brave boy," Phoebe whispered. The van rocked violently as Shorty shifted into gear and they lurched forward. "We're going home. To your new home in Hickory Grove." She smiled at him, squeezing his warm little hand. "You're going to like it there, *sohn*."

By the lights along the highway, Phoebe studied Joshua in the front seat of the van. She had barely recognized him back at her stepfather's farm. He'd seemed so much older than his years. So mature and masculine in a way she hadn't seen him before. She had never thought she wanted to marry so she could have a man to protect her or care for her. She had been looking for those things for John, but hearing Joshua speak up that way to Edom had given her a new appreciation for the idea of having someone to care for her. And for her to have someone to care for besides children.

Joshua spotted her looking at him and he smiled. She glanced away, embarrassed to be caught woolgathering that way.

It was almost ten at night and they had just crossed the state line into Delaware. In a little more than an hour, they would be safely home. Shorty was a good driver. He didn't speed, but he kept to the timetable they had laid out that morning. There had been plenty of rest stops, though they hadn't lingered. Shorty seemed to be as eager to return to Kent County as they were.

Phoebe glanced at Bay in the back. She was lying across the seat, buckled in, using her black wool cloak for a blanket. Next Phoebe's gaze moved to her son. John-John was sound asleep in the car seat, his head tilted back, his mouth slightly open. Occasionally, he moved his lips as if suckling. She smiled and lifted the corner of the quilt her mother had given her to cover him with, tucking it over his shoulder. She'd used it to wrap him up to take him into the rest stops to use the bathroom. He was only just potty trained so she was relieved he had no accidents, otherwise, he would have been wearing nothing but the quilt. She knew she should have been concerned as to what he would wear once they arrived, but she wasn't. Rosemary would find something for him until Phoebe had a chance to make him some shirts and pants. And Bay said Rosemary kept a whole box of hand-me-down boots and shoes, and she was sure something in there would fit John's feet.

Phoebe glanced at Joshua again. This time he was watching her. For a moment, they just sat there, gazing into each other's eyes.

He had told Edom that he intended to marry her. But he'd said nothing to her on the matter on the long ride home, and suddenly she felt like she needed to talk about it. Had he said it just to satisfy her mother or anger Edom? Or was he now having second thoughts after seeing what she had come from? Compared to the life he had led with his father, the life he led now in Hickory Grove, their upbringing was very different. Maybe he wanted someone from a similar background to him.

Phoebe heard a seat belt click and Joshua got up. "Okay if I sit there with you?" he asked quietly.

She nodded, scooting over a little. There were three seat belts across the middle row, though with the car seat it was tight. She looked up at Joshua as he took the seat beside her.

He had removed his Sunday hat hours ago and was now wearing the knit watch cap Rosemary had made for him pulled down over his ears. He'd also taken off his good long wool coat and laid it across the back of the van and replaced it with the gray hoodie he liked to wear. Dressed this way, he seemed more like the Joshua she knew than the one she had seen confront Edom back in New Wilmington.

He settled into the spot beside her, leaving her between him and John's car seat. His body was warm against hers and she had to fight the urge to rest her head on his shoulder.

He fastened his seat belt and took her hand in his.

Phoebe knew she should pull her hand away, but the warmth and strength of his touch felt so good. She nodded, looking up at him. She needed to ask him about what he had said to Edom and her mother about marrying her, but a part of her was afraid to do it. Her mother had put him in an uncomfortable position. What *could* Joshua have said, considering the circumstances? Phoebe knew it wouldn't be fair to hold him to it.

"How are you doing?" he asked softly.

"Okay," she breathed.

He looked past her to where John-John was snoring softly in the car seat. He smiled. "He seems okay. Happy to be with his *mam* again."

"He was a little afraid at first," she said, gazing at her son's beautiful sleeping face. "He's never been in a car seat before. Or a car."

"Never been in a car?" Joshua's brow furrowed. "How is that possible. All the Amish I know use drivers for doctor's appointments and visiting at any distance."

"He's never been anywhere but our farm and the neighbors' for church services," she explained. "He was born in that farmhouse." She pressed her lips together. "Edom liked to keep the children nearby."

Joshua shook his head, seeming to be trying to wrap his head around the idea. "Doctor's appointments? Immunizations?"

"The county sent someone out. Edom doesn't approve of such things, but I insisted. I called and they sent out a nurse."

"That's good," he told her. "Because in Dover all our children are immunized, the same as Englisher children. We've heard of Amish communities where they don't follow the same guidelines and there have been illnesses."

"I know," she said quietly. She didn't want to wake John or Bay. She needed these minutes of privacy with Joshua. "Whooping cough was a problem in our area."

He sighed, looking away, then back at her, still holding her hand. "You don't have to worry about any of that now. John-John's safe with you. Safe with us." He squeezed her hand.

"Joshua." She looked up at him. "What you said when we were leaving." She had to stop for a moment as emotion welled up in her throat. She waited until it passed and then went on, "You were put in a bad position. I want you to know I won't hold you to it."

"Hold me to *what*?"

She groaned. She hated that he was going to make her say it. He always wanted that—for things to be said outright. But a part of her liked it. She had loved John, but they hadn't talked a lot. Not about important things. And there had been misunderstandings. And tears on her part because of them.

"You told my mother and Edom that you were going to marry me. You don't have to do that."

"Of course I do," he said, raising his voice.

She glanced over her shoulder. Bay was still asleep. As was John-John. And Shorty seemed to be paying them no mind. "You don't," she repeated, lowering her voice and hoping he would do the same.

"I do," he argued, letting go of her hand. "I have to marry you because I love you."

Before she could stop him, he went on, "Phoebe, I know you loved John and I can never be him. And I know you don't love me." He took her hand again. "But I think… No, I have faith that in time you'll come to love me, too." He hesitated. "Do you think you could ever love me?"

She reached up and brushed his cheek with her hand. She really hadn't thought she could ever love again. The feelings welling up inside were very different from the ones she had felt for John. But in many ways, looking back, those feelings for John seemed girlish and immature. These feelings she had for Joshua were… She wasn't exactly sure what they were but she had an idea she had told her mother the truth. That she was falling in love with Joshua. And every fiber of her being wanted to tell him so. She wanted to tell him that she would marry him.

The only thing that made her hold back was her son sleeping beside her. Her first responsibility was to John-John. "I do want to marry you," she whispered cautiously. "But I'm not ready to say yes."

"You want to marry me? Really?" He sounded like a little boy so much that it made her smile.

"I do. But I want you to get to know John-John first. You need to be sure you're ready, not just to be my husband, but also his father."

"But we could still be betrothed?" he said hopefully.

"I want to wait. Just a little longer," she assured him. "Because I want you to be sure. And…" She hesitated. "When we do become betrothed, I want to go ahead and set a date with the bishop for the marriage. A woman my age with a child—there should be no long engagement."

He was quiet for a long moment, so long that she feared she'd pushed him too far. But at last he nodded ever so slightly. "I know how I feel, Phoebe. About you. About the boy. But I also understand your hesitation. We'll wait to announce our betrothal."

"We'll wait to *talk* about becoming betrothed," she corrected.

"We'll wait to announce it," he repeated.

She couldn't resist a smile. "We'll wait," she agreed.

He leaned closer to her, presenting his cheek. "You think I could get a kiss to seal the deal?" he asked playfully.

She plucked her hand from his and crossed her arms over her chest. "I already told you, Joshua Miller. You'll not get a kiss from me until our wedding day."

Chapter Nine

Phoebe stood at the kitchen table, her arms aching as she rolled out the last bit of dough for her egg noodles. The entire table was covered with long, flat noodles hanging on drying racks made from wooden dowel rods. She lifted the heavy rolling pin, added a sprinkling of flour and rolled the pin over the dough again. The trick to making noodles was to get the dough nice and thin before cutting it into strips. It was a skill she'd learned from her mother at a young age, and her mother had learned from *her* mother. *If you can make noodles*, her mother used to say, *you'll never go to bed hungry*.

The kitchen was empty, which was unusual for late morning, but all of the women in the family seemed to be about their own business before gathering to prepare and serve the next meal. Bay was at the harness shop restocking shelves of baked goods she and Tara had made the night before. Ginger was working a shift in the back of the shop, repairing a neighbor's harness that had been broken in a fender bender coming out of Byler's store. Nettie and Tara had taken a buggy and gone to Fifer's Orchard to get Granny Smith apples and visit with a friend who worked there. And Rosemary had taken her three boys, Jesse, Josiah and James, to the Fishers to deliver miniloaves of cranberry-nut bread and have a visit. After weeks of being off her feet, Rosemary's doctor had given her permission to begin walking in a shoe with orthopedic support, and she said she felt like a caged singing bird that had finally found her way outside.

Phoebe added a bit more flour to the dough and flipped the piece over. It was nice to have a few minutes to herself to gather her thoughts. Life had been so busy since their return from New Wilmington that she'd barely had time to catch her breath. She had John-John to care for now, plus the rest of her duties here on the farm. It was important to her that she continue to pull her weight in the house. With two more mouths for Rosemary and Benjamin to feed, it only seemed fair that she take on part of the burden of caring for such a large household. And one of the ways she could contribute was a project like this one.

The whole thing started when Phoebe had, on impulse, rolled out some fresh noodles for a chicken soup one day. Everyone had raved about the wide egg noodles, and they wanted them with butter the next night as a side dish. Two days later, they wanted them again. With a family so large, she needed to make a lot of noodles, and letting them dry thrown over bowls and pots wasn't practical. Bay was the one who convinced her they needed freestanding drying racks made from wooden dowels, and then she persuaded Joshua and Jacob to make them. It turned out Bay had ulterior motives for getting the brothers to make the noodle racks. She wanted to bag noodles and sell them in the harness shop in her little baking and preserves area, which seemed to be growing bigger by the week.

Satisfied with the thinness of the dough, Phoebe set aside the wooden rolling pin, picked up a paring knife and began to cut the last of the long strips that would be noodles once they dried. They had to dry, of course, because otherwise they would just be a kind of slippery dumpling. By her calculation, she had enough noodles to bag up a dozen one-pound bags and still be able to make a traditional chicken and noodle dish served over mashed potatoes for family dinner the following day. There was no need to cook tonight because they were all invited to Rosemary's oldest daughter Lovage's home to celebrate her husband's grandmother's birthday. It was to be a big event with standing room only, Lovey had told her at church on Sunday. Her husband Marshall's grandmother, Lynita, had insisted on not only inviting everyone from their church district, but three more districts. It would be a fun family evening with good food and conversation, and Phoebe was looking forward to it.

The back door opened, and Phoebe heard Joshua's voice. She couldn't quite make out what he was saying, but there was no mistaking the peals of laughter coming from her son. A moment later, Joshua walked into the kitchen carrying John-John on his shoulders.

"Duck down!" he warned in English.

The toddler obediently followed Joshua's instruction. The moment her son had entered the house, everyone had begun to teach him English. They still spoke to him in their native language, of course. But Benjamin believed that being bilingual was important to being a part of the community within Kent County, both Englisher and Amish, so Phoebe's little boy began learning at once. And it was no surprise to her that his vocabulary was growing in leaps and bounds.

"Mammi!" John-John cried excitedly when he spotted her. He was still wearing his denim coat, and a knit cap that was identical to Joshua's. His nose was bright red, but he had clearly enjoyed his time outside.

"Sohn," she said, looking up at him sitting on Joshua's shoulders. "Did you see to the corncrib door?"

Joshua looked up at John, repeating her question in Pennsylvania *Deutsch.*

"Yes!" John exclaimed, grinning and clapping his hands together.

"All fixed," Joshua declared.

"Fisxed," John echoed.

"We also put a new laying box in the henhouse, and repaired the milking stool. And we managed to find a few minutes to play with Snowball," Joshua said, swinging John-John off his shoulders and setting him down on his stockinged feet.

They had both left their boots out in the mudroom, as requested by Rosemary. The previous night there had been a little dustup after someone with rather large "man feet," as Rosemary had said, had traipsed through her kitchen, leaving footprints on her freshly mopped floor.

"Who's Snowball?" Phoebe asked, cutting the last strip of noodles in the dough. "Don't tell me Jacob has brought another stray dog home?"

Joshua eyed Phoebe. "Snowball's the kitten Ethan

brought home. Remember? The one I showed you. The albino." He leaned down and John stuck his hand inside Joshua's coat.

Phoebe tucked a lock of hair that had slipped out from beneath her scarf behind her ear. "What are you doing, John?" she asked, first in English and then in Pennsylvania *Deutsch*. She laid noodles over her hand and carried them to the end of the table, looking for an empty space on one of the racks, which wasn't going to be easy to find.

"Katz." John giggled as moved his little hand around inside Joshua coat.

Phoebe raised her eyebrows. "In Joshua's coat?"

"Ya," Joshua said sheepishly. He then slipped his hand inside and produced a tiny bundle of white fur.

"Katz!" John cried, putting out both hands to take the kitten.

"Ne, you can't carry it, right?" Joshua said. "We talked about this, John. If you accidentally drop Snowball, she might be hurt, *ya?"*

"Ya," John agreed, reaching out with one finger to stroke the kitten's back.

"He shouldn't be bringing that kitten in the house," Phoebe chided, finally finding a place to hang the last of the egg noodles. "Rosemary said no more pets in the house. She caught Joshua's dog Silas chewing on James's high chair again."

"But it's just for a few minutes, right?" Joshua asked John. "And then we'll take her back to the barn, yes?"

"Yes!" John declared, his English pronunciation nearly perfect.

"Now, you can hold her, John," Joshua went on, "but

you have to sit down." He walked over to the doorway leading to the hall. "Right here." He waggled his finger. "And you'd best not let her near Rosemary's rag rug because if that *katz* has an accident on that rug, we'll both be in trouble."

Phoebe didn't know how much John understood what Joshua was saying in English, but she laughed and her son laughed with her.

John plopped down on the floor and reached out for the kitten Joshua was holding cradled in his arm.

"Cap," he said, pointing at John's head.

John plucked his hat off his head and handed it to Joshua.

"And unbutton your coat." Joshua gestured with his hand. "Otherwise you'll get overheated. If you get sick, your *mam* will keep you indoors for days, fussing over you."

Again, her son did as he was instructed, and then Joshua squatted down and settled the kitten between the toddler's legs.

Watching the two of them together made Phoebe misty-eyed. Not only had Joshua taken to John-John, but the little boy had taken to him. Which was really quite amazing considering the fact that, in the past, her son had been afraid of men. Any time a man spoke to him, he hid behind her skirts and fussed if she insisted he respond to a question or offer a greeting.

"There you go," Joshua said, patting John on his head. Then he stood and looked to Phoebe.

"Thank you," she murmured, smiling at him.

"You're welcome." He pulled off his hat and stuffed his and John's into his coat pocket. He then swung out of his coat and dropped it over one of the kitchen chairs. "All by yourself, are you?"

She nodded, watching him as he approached her. It was interesting to her that the longer she knew him, the more handsome she thought he was. He had the kindest brown eyes and the most beautiful smile that always seemed just a little mischievous. "It's kind of nice. To have a bit of time to myself."

"Not much of that around here," he agreed, coming to stand in front of her. "Which is something I want to talk to you about."

"Oh?" She wiped her hands on her apron. She imagined she looked a sight, hair coming loose under the scarf she wore over her head and tied at the back of her neck. Her apron was powdered with flour, and it looked like she had maple syrup from the morning's breakfast at the hem of her skirt. "What do you mean?"

He reached out to touch her and she knew she should have stepped back, but she couldn't make herself do it. To her surprise, he just brushed the tip of her nose with his finger.

"Flour," he told her. "Right there." He pointed and grinned. "On your nose."

She laughed and rubbed at her nose, thinking she should be embarrassed. But she wasn't. Not in the least. Life was so easy with Joshua. He was even-tempered, gentle and nonjudgmental. Now that she had gotten to know him, she realized her original fear that he might disapprove of her having John-John was completely unfounded. He truly was a man of faith in the greatest sense of the word. And he led his faithful life not just in word but actions. And that, she knew, was hard to come by. It wasn't that she thought there weren't good people in the world, only that they were so imperfect.

"What did you say you wanted to talk to me about?" she asked, returning to the end of the table to clean up.

He pulled out an end of one of the long benches alongside the table. "You have time to sit down?"

"Not really." She walked over to the kitchen counter and opened a drawer in search of the bench scraper. It was an amazing little rectangle of stainless steel Rosemary introduced her to. It was used to lift sticky dough from a surface or scrape flour off a counter or tabletop. "I've got to figure out somewhere to put all of these noodles to dry and then I need to finish the *schnitz un kepp.* Rosemary left the ham hock on the back of the stove, but I forgot to soak the dried apples overnight." She rolled her eyes. Finally locating the scraper, she returned to the table. "And I've still got the dumplings to make."

"Apple and dumplings? Mmm." Joshua smacked his lips. "You know how to make apple and dumplings? If I'd known that, I'd have asked you to marry me sooner."

She pretended to frown. "I think we'd known each other less than a month the first time you asked me to marry you."

"Did not." He grabbed her hand. "Well, maybe." He tugged on her hand. "Come on. Sit down with me for a minute. I've serious business to discuss with you, and when do we ever get a chance to talk alone?"

She sighed. "Never."

"Just for a few minutes." He pulled the chair at the end of the table out for her. "You've been on your feet since dawn. Sit. You deserve a break once in a while."

"All right, but only for a few minutes." She took

the chair he offered. "And we're not really alone." She nodded in the direction of her John, seated on the floor only a few feet from them. He was lying on his belly, propped up on his elbows, watching the kitten bat at an empty thread spool. She had no idea where he had gotten it, but she suspected from his pocket. Since he was old enough to be off lead strings, he'd been tucking odd bits of this and that into his pockets. She always had to be careful to check them before she washed his pants, otherwise she was liable to wash a shiny rock, a bit of corn string or a cicada shell.

Joshua watched her son. "He's a good boy, Phoebe. Smart. And good-hearted."

The look he had in his eyes was almost that of a proud parent. And suddenly Phoebe's heart swelled with joy. Joshua was going to be an excellent father to John-John, better than she had hoped for because he wasn't going to just accept him as another man's child. John would be Joshua's son.

"He is. And you are a good man," she said softly. "To care for him as you do." She laid her hand down over his, which was resting on the kitchen table. He had nice hands, the hands of a man who worked hard, but also knew how to wash them well and trim his nails.

He shifted his gaze from the little boy and the kitten to Phoebe. "I could sit all day and look into your eyes," he told her. "You have the most beautiful blue eyes. And your hair." He caught another wisp that had escaped her blue scarf and hung across her forehead. "Like honey…spun honey."

Feeling heat in her face, she drew back, lifting her

hand from his. She patted her cheek. "Such nonsense you say."

"Not nonsense," he replied matter-of-factly as he sat back on the bench. "The truth. But enough flirting with me, I have things to tell you."

She chuckled, appreciating that he had lightened the moment. "I was *not* flirting with you."

"Sure you were. Look, you've made me blush." He patted his cheeks. "So, here's what we need to discuss. I want to tell you what I'm thinking, but you have to be honest with me, Phoebe." He leaned forward again, clasped his hands together and rested them on the table between them. "If this won't work for you, just tell me. I'll come up with something else. I promise you."

"Okay…" She drew out the word. She had no idea what he was talking about, but now she was definitely curious to hear it.

He took a deep breath and exhaled. "Bay and I still have to go over some of the details with my *dat*, but it looks like we can break ground on the greenhouse as soon as we get the first thaw in the spring. Mid-March, we're thinking. Our plan is to put up a little makeshift greenhouse for seedlings right away, then we have a little time to build the bigger one. For this year we're thinking we use some of Dat's shop for sales, but we leave room to connect the two buildings later. Build our own sales shop. Bay has it in her head folks will come shopping for plants and wander over to the harness shop for their other needs. Seeds, baked goods, ointments for their livestock, you name it."

She nodded. She didn't know much about the business of sales, but she could tell Joshua had a head for it. And Bay, too. Listening to the two of them go on at the dinner table, she had no doubt they would be successful in their new venture.

"I think we've got a good business model here and I honestly believe that I can make a decent living, what with selling plants and other things. I'm thinking we should go into making little fish ponds and water gardens. Like Rosemary's out back." He knocked on the table with his knuckles. "Englishers like that sort of thing and they'll pay you to put it in, sometimes even to maintain it."

She nodded, enjoying hearing the excitement in his voice.

"But here's the thing," he said, hesitating. "The money I've been saving since I started getting paid to work when I was fourteen, it all needs to go into the business right now. For this growing season. So...what I'm trying to say is that, Phoebe, I can't build a house for us right now. Dat's already offered me a bit of land on the back of the property past the old orchard. It's the perfect place to build a house, but not this year," he finished.

"So you think we should wait a season to be married," she said, trying hard to hide her disappointment. She knew what he was saying made sense, but now that she'd just about made up her mind to marry him, the idea of having to wait a whole year, or maybe longer, was discouraging.

"Ne!" He held up his palm to her. "That's not what I'm saying at all. What I'm saying...what I'm *asking* you, is how you would feel about marrying and living here. Just for a year. Two at most," he added quickly.

"There are more than enough bedrooms in this house that we could have the privacy due a man and wife, and that way we could save money. I don't know if I ever told you this before, but my *dat* and *mam* lived together with her parents for two years before they bought their farm. They always said it worked out just fine. Ethan was born when they were still living there." He exhaled, suddenly looking defeated. "You think it's a terrible idea."

"*Ne, ne,* I don't." She laughed and grabbed his hands. In truth, she was thinking that if they did marry, she would miss the family life here in Rosemary and Benjamin's house. It was a life she had never known, and she wanted John-John to see what it was like to be loved the way Rosemary and Benjamin loved their children. She wanted him to see how a family was supposed to treat each other.

"You don't think it's a terrible idea?" He sat back, relief clear on his face. Then he leaned forward again, his forehead creasing. "You're sure? You're not just saying that?"

She drew her hands from his, wrapping her arms around her waist. "I'm saying what I think. And that's something we should agree on right now, Joshua. That if we marry…we'll always be honest with each other. Even if it means bruising feelings sometimes."

"Wait." He grinned and pointed at her. "So, you're agreeing to marry me?"

"I've agreed to no such thing." She rose from her chair and began to measure out cups of flour into the bowl she'd just used to make the noodles. It would do just fine for the dumplings for the *schnitz un kepp.* She avoided eye contact with him to keep from giggling with happiness.

"But you just said you would be fine with us living here together as man and wife for a year."

"I said," she told him, dumping the fourth cup of flour into the bowl. "That if we married, I thought it would be acceptable. Could you pass me the baking powder?" She pointed at the red can on the table in front of him.

He picked it up but pulled it out of her reach when she tried to take it from him. "Tell me you'll marry me and I'll make the dumplings for you."

"You will do no such thing," she teased. "I can't imagine what your—"

"Mammi!" John-John called from the floor. "My finger!" He jumped up, holding out his index finger for her to see. "Katz licked my finger!"

Phoebe looked at her son, then at Joshua, and then they were all laughing.

Phoebe stood in the doorway of Rosemary's eldest daughter's kitchen and watched John-John jog down the hall in a herd of toddlers. He quacked as he dragged behind himself a wooden duck on the end of a corn string. His newfound friends joined him in a cacophony of barnyard animal sounds. One was pulling a wooden dog, another a cow. There was barking and meowing and mooing, and interestingly enough, the sound of a solitary elephant. "John, no running in the house," she called after him.

When he didn't respond, she made to go after him, but Lynita, Lovey's grandmother-in-law, stepped between them. "Let him go. It's not the first time a boy has run in this house. Won't be the last, I hope. Boys run. It's what they do."

Lynita Byler stood only five feet tall, but she was a hearty-sized woman, round with chubby cheeks and a smile that was infectious. Phoebe didn't know how old she was, despite the fact that they were celebrating her birthday this evening. Lynita had made it plain her age wasn't anyone's business, but Phoebe suspected she was in her early- to mid-seventies.

Lynita studied her from behind her round, wire-frame eyeglasses. "Nice boy, your John, but a bit coddled. I say let him run. If he falls…" She shrugged. "Be there to pick him up. It's how I raised my son, and Marshall, too," she said referring to Lovey's husband. "And Sam."

After the deaths of Marshall and Sam's parents, Lynita had moved in with her grandsons and Marshall had become his little brother's guardian. Then, a little over a year ago, Lovey had married Marshall and they were expecting their first child at any moment.

Phoebe smiled and nodded respectfully. In the community she had come from, all the women wore black prayer *kapps*, but here in Hickory Grove they were reserved for the elders. A woman of Lynita's age and experience was someone all the younger women looked up to. Someone they could all learn from.

"Thank you for inviting us to celebrate your birthday with you," Phoebe said. "Lovey's family, everyone here has been so kind and welcoming."

Lynita frowned. "Not offering any more than you

deserve." She raised a thick, gray eyebrow. "Rosemary tell you I know Edom Wickey?"

Phoebe shook her head no.

"Through a cousin's daughter. Not well, but well enough to know what kind of man he is. Well enough to know you deserve every kindness we can offer you. More. I'm just thankful you were able to get yourself and that son of yours out of that house. I— Don't let those boys touch that cake!" she hollered into the sitting room. She looked back at Phoebe. "I best go rescue my birthday cake. Made it myself. Rainbow sprinkles. You had them? They sell them at Byler's."

Phoebe pressed her lips together to keep from giggling. "I've seen them. Never had them."

"Well, you're in for a treat. Taste like coconut candy. Mary Elise! Don't you let them put their fingers in that cake!" Lynita hustled through the doorway, her short arms pumping.

Smiling to herself, Phoebe walked back to the kitchen, thinking she would get a start on the mountains of dirty dishes piled on the countertops. Lovey had said they could wait, that she and Marshall would *ret* them up after everyone went home, but Phoebe thought she would at least get a start on them.

Lovey had put on quite a spread. Besides making chicken and dumplings, Lynita's favorite, there had been broccoli, coleslaw, green beans and yeast bread. And as if that wasn't enough, there had also been pickled beets, mashed potatoes and homemade applesauce. Phoebe had eaten until she was stuffed. And there was still the rainbow sprinkle cake to be served along with homemade cinnamon doughnuts, *rahmpudding* and huckleberry streusel.

At the sink, she had just filled the dishpan with soapy hot water when she heard someone walk into the kitchen. A man, by the sound of the footsteps.

"There you are."

Her first thought when she had heard the footsteps was that it was Joshua and she had already started to spin around to greet him. But as the man spoke, she realized it wasn't Joshua.

It was Eli standing in the doorway.

"Oh," she said, her smile fading. Then, realizing how that must look, she offered the best smile she could muster. "Eli." She hoped she didn't sound too disappointed. He was such a nice man. She didn't want to hurt his feelings.

"I thought you might be hiding in here." He walked into the kitchen, seeming quite at ease, which surprised her. Most men weren't comfortable in any woman's kitchen but their mothers' and their wives'.

"I was...starting the dishes. Washing." She pointed lamely at the dishpan of sudsy water.

"I can see that." He chuckled. "I've washed a few dishes myself. It's where I start, too." He pointed. "With dirty dishes, clean water and dish detergent."

She dried her hands on her apron. Despite him trying to make a joke, she felt awkward there alone with him. The other times they had talked, they had always been surrounded by other people. "You've washed dishes?"

"Ya." He walked closer, sliding his hands casually into his pants pockets. She could see that he'd recently trimmed his beard. Unlike many men his age, which

had to be more than thirty, he didn't let his beard grow long and scraggly. His hair was also neatly trimmed. And he looked to be wearing a new shirt because the blue hadn't faded yet, a blue close to the color of the sky.

"As I told you, I'm a single man. With four children to care for." He smiled kindly. "Someone's got to wash dishes. Lizzy's not tall enough yet." He chuckled. Another joke.

Phoebe smiled, feeling self-conscious. "Right, I guess I was just thinking…your mother, you said she was living with you."

"*Ya*, she is, but…not to be unkind, but she's not a lot of help. She does what she can, but she's elderly and has a bad hip, and really, why should my mother still be washing my dishes and my clothes? She did that for me the first twenty-five years of my life."

Phoebe nodded thoughtfully. He had a good point. And she liked the fact that he didn't think that just because his mother was a female, she was responsible for the household chores.

"Which leads me," Eli said slowly, "to a question I have for you."

Phoebe felt the blood drain from her face. She immediately knew what was coming. He still hadn't given up the idea of walking out with her. She had hoped Eli would just let it go, but obviously he wasn't going to. Her next hope was that someone would come into the kitchen and save both her and Eli from this awkwardness, but she could hear the birthday guests laughing and chatting in the other rooms of the house. She doubted either of them was going to be rescued. She exhaled, meeting Eli's gaze. "*Ya*, Eli. What do you want to ask me?"

"I think you know." He took a step closer.

He smelled of soap and laundry detergent. A clean smell that was pleasant. But it didn't make her light-headed the way Joshua did when he stepped too close to her. "Eli," she said softly, already feeling bad.

"I want to ask you again if I can court you."

"Eli," she said again. "I know that you think—"

"*Ne.*" He held up his finger. "Hear me out, Phoebe. Now that you've brought your son to Hickory Grove, you must know you can't stay under Benjamin's roof forever. I understand he's a hospitable man, but—"

"Joshua Miller has asked me to marry him," she blurted.

Eli blanched. "I see." He paused, staring at the floor for a moment, then went on, "Did you..." He lifted his gaze until it met hers. "Have you accepted?"

"I... Not yet, but...I care for him," she finally said.

Eli thought for a moment. "Phoebe, Joshua is a nice boy, but he's just that. A boy. He doesn't have the experience to join two families together." He threaded his fingers together. "Your situation...with John, it would be better accepted in the community, were you married to a man a bit older, a man with children, a man..." He exhaled, seeming to be searching for the right words. "A man who understands that we all sin and can accept others' failings."

"John-John isn't a failing," she said tersely.

He hesitated. "Maybe I could have chosen a better word. I don't always say things the right way, Phoebe, but...I would be a better choice for you as a husband.

And I can promise you that your past would never come between us. Your son would be my son the moment we were wed and I would never treat him differently than my own children."

"Oh, Eli." She looked away, then back to him. "I'm sorry but I can't," she said softly. "I have...*feelings* for Joshua."

Again he met her gaze. And she felt bad because she could see his disappointment in his eyes.

"I appreciate your honesty," he said at last. "And...I won't pester you, but, Phoebe, I want you to know that I'm not taking back my offer. If you change your mind—and I think you will—my offer still stands. I want to marry you. I'd have the banns cried on Sunday if you'd have me."

Phoebe clasped her hands, staring at the floor. She knew Eli was right. He would make a good husband, a good father. But her heart already belonged to Joshua. "Thank you, Eli." She looked up. "I'll not forget your kindness."

He walked out of the room, his footsteps seeming to echo in the kitchen. As Phoebe watched him go, she prayed she had not made a terrible mistake.

Chapter Ten

A customer's harness in hand, Joshua halted at the closed door to his father's workshop. Bay had said she'd just seen him heading that way, so Joshua was fairly certain he was inside. It was odd that the door was closed, though. Benjamin never closed his door, his way of welcoming any children or stepchildren or friends or neighbors at any time of the day.

"Dat?" Joshua called hesitantly. "You in there?"

"Jacob?" came his father's voice from the other side of the door.

"*Ne*, it's Joshua," he replied. It didn't bother him that his father couldn't tell his voice from his twin brother's. There were a lot of folks that couldn't look at them and distinguish one from the other. According to Rosemary, *all* of her stepsons sounded alike, and she claimed she couldn't tell the difference between them if she wasn't face-to-face.

"Come in!" his father called.

Joshua opened the door and walked into the workshop where his father was spending hours each day making his very first buggy, start to finish. Joshua found him seated on a stool at a workbench against the wall. He was wearing a pair of wire-frame eyeglasses he used for close work.

"Close the door." His father waved at him, leaning to peer behind him. "I don't want Rosemary snooping around."

"Snooping?" Joshua asked, pushing the door shut with his foot. "What would she be doing snooping around your workshop? Besides, she went to Lovey's. She's not back yet."

"Don't want to risk it," Benjamin said. "You know how women can be. Eyes in the backs of their heads! Come see what I'm making for her. It's a Christmas present." He beamed.

"A Christmas present?" Joshua was surprised because his father and Rosemary didn't, to his knowledge, exchange gifts. Gifts were not exchanged in Amish homes the way they were in Christian Englisher homes. Like most Amish families, while the Millers did recognize the day, it was a quiet affair spent in family prayer followed by supper. Small children often received a single gift of a homemade toy, or a new pair of mittens, wrapped in brown paper and twine, but that was usually the extent of it. Although, the previous Christmas, Rosemary had surprised everyone with new flannel scarves she'd made, as well as a stack of puzzles she'd bought at Spence's Bazaar. They had spent the evening, after supper, putting puzzles together and drinking hot chocolate and eating cookies. It had been one of the finest Christmases Joshua could remember.

Joshua carefully hung the portion of the broken harness Lee Bontrager had just brought by over a ladder-back chair that needed a new cane seat and approached his father's workbench.

"It's a little stand for her prayer *kapp*," Benjamin explained, his voice filled with enthusiasm.

He had taken a block of gorgeous walnut, sanded it smooth, placed a thick dowel rod in the center and then attached a smaller block on top. Joshua didn't know of any women who had such a stand, but then as a single man, he didn't know the details of a woman's life behind her bedroom door. What he *did* know was how precious an Amish woman's prayer *kapp* was to her and how well she cared for it. In his entire life he had never once seen his *mam*'s or Rosemary's or one of his sisters' *kapps* lying on a counter or table, or even dangling from the clothesline. Women wore their *kapps* most of their waking hours and when they weren't wearing them, they were stored carefully in their bedrooms. The *kapps* were rarely washed, but when they were, they were stuffed with paper to dry and then starched back into perfect shape.

"I'm thinking about adding a light stain," Benjamin said, thinking aloud. "Then a couple of coats of poly. I'll do a fine sand between each coat, of course."

"It's beautiful, Dat," Joshua said. "Rosemary will love it."

Benjamin shrugged. "It's been a hard year for her, what with the little ones getting more active and then her foot surgery. I wanted to have something nice for her."

Joshua slid his hands into his pockets, thinking to himself that when he and Phoebe were married, he might make her a stand to hold her prayer *kapp* as a gift. He couldn't think of anything more fitting for a husband to give a wife. He could just imagine what it would look like on top of the dresser in their bedroom.

"It's a nice piece, Dat."

Benjamin sat back, nodding as he studied his handiwork. "*Ya*, I think it— Oh, wait. I forgot to show you the best part." Brushing away sawdust, he reached across the workbench and picked up an object the size of a quarter.

Joshua stepped closer to get a better look. His father held a delicate carving of a rosebud in the palm of his hand.

"Made from rosewood," Benjamin said, proudly. "Got the wood from the chair shop over at Seven Poplars. Carved it myself."

"It's beautiful, Daddi."

"A rosebud, you know, for my rosebud," his father went on to explain, his cheeks reddening. "I'm going to glue it right here." He indicated the center of the block of wood that rested on the bottom. "I think the rosewood will make a nice contrast against the walnut."

Joshua nodded, taking a step back, slipping his hands into his pockets again. At first, his father's open affection for Rosemary had made him and his brothers a bit uncomfortable, but now that he had gotten used to it, he liked it. He liked the fact that his father was a man who could show some emotion in a culture where it was never encouraged, even frowned upon. And now that he knew what it felt like to love a woman, to love Phoebe, he understood his father's desire to express his feelings for his wife. When he had fallen in love with

Phoebe, it had all made sense to him. So many things in the world made sense to him now.

Wanting to lighten the moment, Joshua pointed to the delicately carved piece. "A bit fancy, though, wouldn't you say. What will the bishop think?" he teased his father.

Benjamin smiled. "I don't expect Bishop Simon to ever have need to be in our bedroom, do you?" He shrugged. "I doubt he'll ever know about it. And if he does and he takes issue, he and I will sit down and talk about what the good Lord has to say about a husband caring for his wife."

Joshua didn't doubt his father could take on their bishop, quoting Bible verse. It wasn't unusual for Amish men and women not to be well-read in the Bible. Many folks thought that was best left to the preachers and the bishops, but it was his father's belief that any man who had a head for the Lord's word should be familiar with it, so he could share them with others. Friends and neighbors sometimes came to Benjamin about religious matters rather than to their preacher. It happened so often that there was talk he might be the next preacher in their church district.

Remembering what he'd come for in the first place, Joshua reached for the harness that he'd left on the chair. "I wanted you to have a look at this breastplate. Lee Bontrager thinks it can be repaired." He grimaced. "But I think not. I think it needs to be replaced. He said I should ask you, though." He cast a sideways glance at his father. "I guess he doesn't think I know what I'm talking about? I've only been working in your harness shop since I was ten."

Benjamin chuckled and reached out to run a finger along the leather that was near cut through. "Lee means well. Doesn't always think through how things he says might be taken." He took a closer look, pushing his eyeglasses up on his nose. "What happened to it? It looks like a rat has been chewing on it."

"Lee didn't say," Joshua answered. "I thought the same, but it's not like one man wants to tell another he's got a problem with rats in his barn."

Benjamin shrugged. "True, but it's not as if we haven't all run into it one time or another. It's his dislike of cats that's the problem. Last year, he had rats after his guinea hens. I keep saying, 'Lee, what you need is a couple of barn cats.' But he won't hear of it." He ran his fingers over the leather once more. "*Ne*, I'll not fix that. It will only come unsewn again and then I'll look like I don't know what I'm doing. Tell him it will have to be replaced."

"Will do."

"And tell him he needs a cat," Benjamin added, pointing his finger at his son.

"Right." Joshua chuckled as he headed for the door. Lee was waiting for him in the shop. He was chatting with Bay when he left him.

Joshua had just reached the door when his father called back to him.

"Wait, Joshua. I meant to speak to you about something, when I had you alone."

Joshua turned back to him, the harness in his hands. "*Ya*, Dat?"

"The girl." His father suddenly sounded hesitant, as if he had a mind to say something but didn't want to.

He removed his eyeglasses and set them on the workbench. "Phoebe."

Joshua suddenly got a sick feeling in the pit of his stomach. "What of her?"

"I'm not exactly sure how to say this. I mean no ill will to her. I just—" Benjamin sighed. "I think… Son, you've been kind to her. A good friend, and you've been so good to the boy, but I—" He looked up at Joshua. "I think you should take a step back."

Joshua narrowed his gaze. "A *step back*? What do you mean?"

"I guess what I'm trying to say is that a little distance between you two might be good right now. Because she seems to be, well, taken with you."

Joshua was silent. He wondered how much his father knew about him and Phoebe? But what *could* he know? Joshua had said nothing of his anticipated engagement with Phoebe, and he knew very well that Phoebe hadn't said anything to anyone. She was the one who wanted to wait. Bay and Jacob were probably suspicious, but they would never have gone to their father without coming to Joshua first.

His father groaned. "I hate to say this, but I'm worried she might get the wrong idea."

Joshua heard the metal rings of the harness clink together in his hands. "And what idea is that?" he asked, emphasizing each word.

"Sohn, I know you know she came to Hickory Grove to look for a husband. And I have no problem with that." He held his hand up, palm out. "When Rosemary asked me about having Phoebe here, I didn't balk. Not for one second. It was the right thing to do, her being related to

Rosemary and all. And to give the girl a place to start over. But…"

Joshua clenched his jaw. He was beginning to realize what his father was trying to say, but there was a stubbornness in him that made him want to hear it out of his father's own mouth. "Exactly what are you worried about, Dat?" he asked, trying to keep the anger he was feeling in his chest out of his voice.

"I'm worried that she might get the wrong impression. That she might think you're sweet on her, too," he blurted, his face reddening.

"Sweet on her?" Joshua repeated.

"Ya." His father sighed, seeming genuinely relieved his son understood him. "That's what I'm saying. It's not fair to a girl to make her think, make her *hope*, that you might have interest in her beyond…well, beyond the same interest the whole family has in her. You wouldn't want Phoebe to think that you might consider walking out with her."

Joshua squared his shoulders. "But I *do* want to walk out with her. In fact, I was just about to come speak with you about going to the bishop with me. Dat, I don't just want to walk out with Phoebe, I want to *marry* her."

The blood seemed to drain from his father's face. One moment it had been bright red and now suddenly he was pale. "You…" He looked down at the poured concrete floor as he rose from his stool. "*Sohn*, you can't marry her," he said quietly. "I forbid it."

Joshua just stood there in shock, his hands slowly falling until they rested on his thighs. The harness hung from his fingers, brushing the floor, the chain jingling. "What do you mean you *forbid* it?"

His father dragged his hand across his mouth and then slowly lifted his gaze until he met Joshua's. "I know you know what her circumstances are. The boy…"

Joshua was embarrassed to realize that he was close to tears. He hadn't cried since he was eleven when he fell out of the loft chasing Jacob and had broken his arm. But there was also a ripple of anger rising him. Right now, it was in the pit of his stomach, but he could feel it intensifying. He shook his head, taking a deep breath. "But, Dat, she *confessed* her sin."

"I understand that," his father hedged. "But…" He drew his hand across his mouth again. "You're still so young, Joshua. A woman of that nature, she…" He groaned. "Men don't marry women like that."

"But you said she came here to find someone to marry." He gestured lamely. "You agreed to have her living here with us, knowing she was looking for a husband."

"A husband, yes, just not one of my sons."

"Because of her sin?" Joshua asked, raising his voice an octave. As he spoke he dropped Lee's harness on the back of the chair waiting to be reupholstered. "That's what you mean?"

"Ya," Benjamin said, his voice getting louder. "That's what I mean."

Joshua was flabbergasted to hear his father say such a thing. "But we're forgiven of our sins if we ask for forgiveness, isn't that what our bishop tells us? What our preachers preach?"

"Yes, yes of course," Benjamin replied, taking a step toward his son. "But—"

"But what?" Joshua asked. "Either we are forgiven

and welcomed back into the fold or we are not. Which is it?"

"Of course we're forgiven. Phoebe is forgiven. She's obviously a godly woman. And I like her. I genuinely do."

"Just not for me?" Joshua asked, taking a step back toward the door.

"Just not for you," Benjamin said, getting louder. "No son of mine will marry a woman like that!"

Joshua just stood there staring at his father for a moment. There was a part of him that wanted to shout back at his father that he loved Phoebe, and he was fairly certain she loved him. That he was going to marry her. He was going to be her husband, and he was going to be John-John's father. That he was an adult and he had the right to choose who he would marry. That he wasn't asking his father's permission. But something ingrained in him restrained him. Never had he and his father had a fundamental disagreement like this. And he was still his father. He had raised Joshua to respect his parents in all matters.

Joshua turned around abruptly and strode toward the door. "I have to go," he said, afraid that if he didn't go, he might say something he'd regret later.

"Son, I know you're upset, but it's better if—"

Joshua yanked open the door. Halfway through, he realized he had left Lee Bontrager's harness over the chair, but he couldn't bring himself to go back for it. He was too upset, too angry, too sad. Sad that all of his plans may just have gone out the window.

* * *

"Phoebe?" Joshua's voice came from the top of the steps to the entrance to the cellar.

She was in the middle room of the below-ground cellar where Rosemary stored her root vegetables. Lined on both sides of the brick walls were shelves filled with jars of preserved fruits and vegetables. There were quart jars of spiced peaches and applesauce and green beans and stewed tomatoes and fruit compote, along with all manner of preserves like blackberry and blueberry and strawberry. Below the shelves, along the floor, were bushel and half-bushel-sized baskets of three kinds of potatoes, carrots, beets, rutabagas and turnips. She'd come down in search of a small basket of multicolored creamer potatoes Tara was certain were stored there.

Phoebe heard Joshua coming down the wooden stairs, his boots heavy on the wooden treads. She wondered what he was doing around the house this time of day. He was supposed to be working a shift in the harness shop. She couldn't imagine business was so slow that he had time to sneak a few minutes alone with her. Which wasn't a good idea, anyway. He'd tried to kiss her the night before when they'd bumped into each other in the hall in the darkness and she'd almost succumbed. Had it not been for the sound of James's and John-John's laughter in the bathroom where they were splashing water instead of washing their hands, she might have broken her promise to herself that there would be no kiss between them until they were man and wife.

"Tara said there were potatoes down here, but I can't find them," she said as much to herself as him.

"There you are." His voice sounded strained.

"The potatoes are small," she explained, showing him something the diameter of a quarter with her thumb and forefinger. She leaned down and moved another half bushel of potatoes, wondering if the ones she was looking for were hidden behind them. "They're red and purple and white. Not the long ones. Like the ones we had in the beef stew the other day," she went on, annoyed she couldn't find them. She hated to bother Tara, who was busy in the kitchen cutting up cabbage, but if she couldn't find them herself, she supposed she'd have to go back upstairs and—

"I need to talk to you," Joshua said.

The tone of his voice and the way it quivered made Phoebe's heart sink. A sudden rush of thoughts overwhelmed her.

He had changed his mind about wanting to marry her.

She'd not accepted yet. Which had given him time to rethink the matter.

And now her heart was going to be broken.

But better now than later down the road, she told herself, preparing for him to speak the words. Better just her heart than John-John's, too.

She stiffened, took a breath and steeled herself for Joshua's admission. And tried to hold back tears. A part of her was proud that he had the nerve to tell her now, before their engagement became public. He wasn't just saving face, he was sparing her, too.

"What is it?" she asked softly. She looked up to find him in the doorway of the little room, his hand pressed to the wall. She lowered her gaze, fighting tears even though he hadn't even said it yet.

He pulled off his black knit cap and balled it in his fist. "I've just come from speaking with my father, and—" He exhaled. His voice was still trembling. "I'm sorry, Phoebe, but—"

She could feel her tears stinging the backs of her eyelids. It will be all right, she told herself. *God in His wisdom has a plan for me. God has a plan for all of us. Sometimes we just don't see it at first.*

"You've changed your mind," she finished for him. Even though she tried to keep the emotion out of her voice, she didn't quite succeed.

"My *dat*—" He looked up suddenly, took a step toward her and grasped both her arms. "Phoebe, *ne*. I haven't changed my mind about you. What would make you think that?"

She sniffed, gazing into his eyes. "You *haven't*?" she breathed, half afraid to believe what he was saying.

"*Ne*, of course not. I meant what I said when I told you I wanted to marry you. I love you, Phoebe. It's only that when we wed…we can't stay here."

"Ah, your father thinks there's not room?" She gave a little laugh, feeling almost weak at the knees. She had been so afraid he didn't love her, just now when she was beginning to accept that she loved him. "That's fine," she said with great relief. "We can wait to be married. I know I said I wanted to marry with haste. But we can wait. And if I've outstayed my welcome, I'm sure I can stay elsewhere. With Lovey or maybe—"

"Phoebe," he interrupted. "I don't know how to say this. But my father doesn't want me to marry you."

"What?" she asked, completely taken by surprise. And then she felt her heart tumbling again. Her stomach lifted to her throat and for a moment she thought she might be sick. "Because of John-John," she murmured.

He pressed the heel of one hand to his forehead. "We can't stay here after we wed because my father doesn't want us to marry," he said, not seeming to have heard her. "But we'll figure this out, Phoebe. My uncle, Abraham, he has a dairy farm and a mill. In upstate New York. My *mam*'s brother. I know he would hire me. We…" He let go of her and began to pace in the small area between a line of baskets of turnips and baskets of carrots. "I'll find us a place to live. There are a lot of people selling properties up there. Amish. We might be able to rent for a while. Maybe look after a place until it's sold. I've seen it done before."

Phoebe barely heard anything he was saying. She was shocked by Joshua's news. Shocked that a man like Benjamin would forbid his son to marry a woman in her circumstances. He had always seemed so liberal to her for a conservative Amish man of his age. And so kind and forgiving. Never would it have occurred to her that he would take such a stance.

Joshua was still going on about his uncle.

"Joshua," she interrupted, reaching out to stop him as he walked by her again. "Tell me the truth. Did your father forbid you to marry me because I committed a sin? Is that what this is about?"

He tried to move away from her, but she caught his arm and tugged, forcing him to look at her. "Is that what happened?" she asked him, hoping beyond hope that wasn't what took place. Knowing it was.

He set his jaw. "My father can't forbid me to do anything. I'm a grown man. I have the right to marry any woman I want. And you're a woman of good standing in the church." He gestured wildly with his hand. "Even the most conservative bishop could put up no argument against our marriage."

"But Benjamin doesn't *want* you to marry me," she said softly.

He hesitated. "*Ne*, he does not," he finally said.

She let go of him and walked away.

"He doesn't, Phoebe. But he'll come around, and if he doesn't," Joshua flung, "then we'll just move away. We'll marry here, and you and John-John and I will start a new life in New York."

"Joshua, I can't do this," she heard herself say. Suddenly chilled to the very bone, she wrapped her arms around her waist, wishing she had worn her wool shawl. She turned to face him, studying him in the dim light that poured from the ground-level half windows on both sides of the room. "I *won't* do this."

"What do you mean? You won't do what?" His voice filled with emotion. Emotions she could only guess at: anger, disappointment, sadness and maybe even fear.

"I won't marry you," she told him.

"Phoebe—"

"Let me have my say, Joshua," she told him firmly. Then she took a moment before she went on. "Your father and your family, they all love you so much. And you need them." She took a step closer to him. She could see he was almost as close to tears as she was. But she didn't see that as weakness. In fact, it made her love him all the more, even knowing their love would never be fulfilled now by the ties of marriage. "I don't think you realize how blessed you are to have such a loving, kind family that cares so much for you. But I know, because I've seen both sides. I've seen the grain and the chaff of the wheat. And you must believe when I say—"

Her voice caught in her throat and she was quiet for a moment. When she had gained control of her emotions again, she went on, "You need them, Joshua. *We* would need them to make our marriage a good one. Because marriage is work, hard work, and a husband and wife need support. They need the love of their family." She shook her head, knowing what she said was right. "I won't come between you and your father. Between you and your family. If I do, you'll hate me someday for it. *Ne*, I'd rather go home to my mother's house with John-John than do this to you. I'd rather marry Eli. I'd rather do anything than put you in this position."

"Go back to Edom? That's ridiculous to say," he told her.

"Well, I can't stay here now, not knowing your father—" She squeezed her eyes shut for a moment and then opened them. "It wouldn't be right for me to stay now."

"I won't hear this." He shook his head obstinately. "You say my father loves me? How can you say that when he would try to keep us apart?"

She smiled sadly. "He thinks he's doing the right thing," she murmured.

"But he isn't!" He drew the back of his hand across his eyes.

"But he *thinks* he is. And that's all a parent can do, Joshua. *Try* to do what's right by their children." She let her arms fall to her sides. "I'm sorry, Joshua," she said, making herself go on even though she didn't want to. "But I cannot—I *will not*—marry you under these conditions. I will not be the one who separates you from your family, because I know what it's like to be alone in the world. And I won't do that to you."

"Phoebe, please." He took a step toward her. "Don't do this. I love you. I want to marry you. I could never marry another woman."

She pressed her lips together to keep them from trembling. "Someone else will come along."

"*Ne!* I could never love anyone but you!"

"Joshua, there's not just one person for each of us. You showed me that," she told him, looking into his beautiful dark eyes, eyes she knew she would never gaze into again. Not the way she was looking at him now. "You just have to trust in God. He'll show you the way."

He took a shuddering breath. "You won't marry me against my father's wishes. Is that what you're saying?"

"That's what I'm saying."

He reached out and stroked her cheek. His fingertips were warm on her cool skin and so gentle. His touch was so loving.

Phoebe closed her eyes, trying to imprint on her memory this moment because she knew she would never feel his touch again. "I'm sorry," she said. Then she opened her eyes and fled, nearly reaching the top of the stairs before she dissolved into tears.

Phoebe stood at the back door of the house and sobbed into her hands. The cold wind of an incoming storm whipped at her skirt and apron. She was so cold. But she couldn't go inside and let anyone see her like this. Her plan was to have a good cry and then go back to the kitchen like nothing had happened. They could pretend nothing had happened because no one knew Joshua had proposed and she had nearly accepted. Well, obviously Benjamin knew, which meant Rosemary knew, but they wouldn't say anything to their children. Phoebe knew they wouldn't do anything to make this harder on Joshua than it had to be, because those were the kind of parents they were.

She took a shuddering breath. When she'd run up the cellar steps, Joshua had followed her. But she'd hidden behind a big old boxwood near the back porch of the house. He'd gone right past and into the house, only to come right back out again when he couldn't find her. When she last saw him, he was heading toward the harness shop.

He just needed some time, she told herself. Once he calmed down, he would understand why she had broken off things with him. He'd accept it.

And in time she, too, would come to accept it. Because it was the right thing to do. She could never have lived with herself if she came between him and his family.

She sniffed and wiped her nose with the hem of her apron. She had no handkerchief.

Now what was she going to do? she wondered as she watched Silas and Adah trotting across the grass side by side. The Chesapeake Bay retrievers had grown since her arrival. They were nearly full-size now, and better behaved. Adah caught sight of her behind the bush and veered off, heading directly for her. Silas followed.

"Go away," she whispered when Adah nuzzled her with her cold nose. "Shoo!" The dog dropped down beside her and she patted her head, actually glad for the company. She sighed and looked out into the empty barnyard.

She had told Joshua she'd return to her mother's house, to Edom's house, but he was right, she couldn't do that. Edom would never take her in again, and even if he was willing to take her, it wouldn't be safe. Not for John-John and certainly not for her. He'd already tried to take her son away from her once. What would prevent him from trying it again?

Taking deep breaths to calm herself, she tried hard to think. She really couldn't stay here now and see Joshua every day. It would be too hard for him, too hard for her. And it wouldn't be the right thing to do to John-John. He was already so attached to Joshua. Leaving now would be hard enough.

Hugging herself for warmth, she leaned against the side of the house. Inside, she could hear the muffled voices of Tara and Nettie. She couldn't tell what they were saying, but they were laughing. They had no idea that her life had just crumbled to pieces. And they wouldn't know, because she could keep it from them.

She just needed a plan. She needed a place to go.

But who would have her? She couldn't go to Lovey. That wouldn't be fair to the family and it wouldn't be a clean break from Joshua.

Then it came to her and she knew instantly what the solution was. She dried her eyes with a clean bit of her apron. She was sure she would be able to borrow a buggy for a short time. She'd clean up and take the buggy and go, now before she weakened. Now while she still had the emotional strength to do it.

Chapter Eleven

When Joshua couldn't find Phoebe, he decided to take a walk to the orchard and back to calm down and get his head on straight. He was so upset, so angry, so hurt and sad that he didn't know what to do about any of this mess. Hands deep in his denim pants pocket, he strode head down into the wind.

How had everything gone so wrong so quickly? He had woken this morning so happy, so excited about his future, his and Phoebe's. And now all those plans seemed to be falling apart right in front of him. Joshua knew he needed to do something, he just didn't know what. He didn't know how to get Phoebe to agree to marry him. He didn't know what to do with his anger with his father. He respected his father so much that he had always hoped he could be just half the man his father was, half the father, half the husband. He could hardly believe that had been his father, the man he loved and admired, standing there in his shop forbidding him to marry the woman he loved.

Joshua walked all the way to the rear of the property,

beyond the old orchard, to the acre of land his father had promised to give him when he married someday. He'd already started planning the layout of the house he would build for himself and Phoebe and John, and the children he hoped God would bless them with. His dream to own a greenhouse and shop, marry Phoebe and live here in Hickory Grove had been so close he had practically tasted it.

And now his dream was in shambles.

The bitter wind found its way down the back of his coat, making him shiver, and he turned around to head back toward the shop. He needed to get back to work. Bay was probably wondering where he was, annoyed that he'd left in the middle of his shift. For all he knew, Lee Bontrager was still waiting to hear the verdict on his harness.

Joshua flipped up the collar of his coat, pulled his knit cap down farther over his ears and, head down again, put one foot in front of the other. *What now?* he kept asking himself over and over again. *What now?* Did he wait for Phoebe to calm down and then try to talk to her again? Did he try to get a hold of his uncle and find out if there was a job for him in New York and *then* try to talk to Phoebe? His uncle had a phone at the mill because he had Englisher customers, too. Maybe if Joshua went to Phoebe with a job in hand, she might agree to marry him and move to New York. Joshua definitely preferred Delaware over New York, but right now he'd live anywhere on the planet to be with Phoebe.

In ordinary circumstances, if he had a problem, his father was the person he would have gone to. His father was good about offering advice without making a man feel foolish, even when he'd done or said a foolish thing. His father had always been the person who had been there for him when he was a child and later had helped him navigate the world of a young Amish man. His father was always a good listener and he always had sound advice to offer.

So, who did Joshua go to now? Now, when it was his father who was the cause of his problem? Sure, Phoebe had said she wouldn't marry him, but that was because of his father. And as much as he hated to admit it, he understood what Phoebe was saying. He understood where she was coming from because of the difficult life she had led. He didn't agree with her, because he *would* leave his family if it meant being able to marry her. It would hurt him, but he was willing to do it. Maybe because, in time, he knew his father would come around. Even welcome them home to Hickory Grove, he suspected. Or at least he hoped that was what would happen.

But Phoebe was a stubborn woman. That was one thing he'd learned early on about her. She never gave up on a task, no matter how hard it was. Her determination was endless. It was how she'd been able to get through the death of the man she had loved, through being a single mother. And once she set her mind on something, she was hard to budge.

He exhaled, and clouds of white formed in front of his face and rose above his head before dissipating. He desperately needed advice, but he didn't know to who to go to. His older brother Ethan, maybe? Ethan was a good man. Like their father, he was wise in most circumstances, but Joshua didn't like the idea of going to him with a problem of the heart. The loss of his wife was still too raw. Joshua didn't want to be the cause of additional pain.

Did he go to Bishop Simon? Did he tell him what his father had said and maybe ask him to intervene? It seemed like a reasonable option, but would that be right to do? Wouldn't that, in a way, be tattling on his father? Was it his place as a son to tell their bishop that Benjamin Miller wasn't following the word of God as it was meant to be?

Joshua kicked a rotten, half-frozen apple as he walked through the overgrown orchard. The old apple- and pear-tree branches hung over his head, bare and skeletal. How, he wondered, could he have been so happy only a few hours ago and now so miserable. How could things have gone so wrong?

After Phoebe had told him she wouldn't marry him, she'd run off. When he heard her crying, he'd gone after her to comfort her, to try to talk some sense into her. But he hadn't been able to find her. She'd been at the top of the cellar steps one moment, the next she was gone. He'd looked for her but to no avail. Tara and Nettie said they hadn't seen her since she went to the cellar and he'd made a quick escape from the kitchen.

By now, he imagined Phoebe would be back in the kitchen helping to prepare supper. Like him, maybe she'd just needed a few minutes alone to collect herself. Now that he had better control of his emotions, maybe they could talk about their situation. There *had* to be a way to be together. If she didn't want to go to New York, maybe he could find a job here in Kent County. He knew an Amish man, Gideon Esch, who owned a scrapple and sausage shop in Dover. He was expanding his business, and every time Joshua went in to pick up an order for Rosemary, Gideon offered him a job. Joshua didn't know anything about sausage making, but he was sure he could learn.

He crammed his hands deeper into his pockets. If his father couldn't approve his marriage, he'd marry Phoebe without his approval and just gain it later. His father was too sensible a man to let this get between them for any length of time. Joshua was sure of it. But he had to convince Phoebe of that.

Joshua was just entering the barnyard when he heard a horse and buggy coming up the lane toward the house. He looked up to see Rosemary approaching in one of the large family buggies, Jesse peeking out of the front window. Slowly he walked toward them as she reined in the horse. When she came to a stop, she opened the door.

"I'll put her up for you," Joshua offered, catching Toby's halter with his fingers. He was always surprised when Rosemary took his father's gelding out instead of one of the quieter horses. Toby was good with a buggy, smart, but he could get frisky at a stop sign and he was a horse that liked speed. He wasn't the kind of horse most women would choose. But then Rosemary wasn't most women, was she?

"Have a good visit with Lovey?" he asked her, trying to hide the myriad of emotions he was feeling at that moment.

Jesse jumped out of the buggy, slammed the door and took off across the barnyard for the house.

Rosemary glanced Jesse's way, then back at Joshua. "Bathroom. I keep telling the boy to tend to his business before he gets in the buggy." She shook her head. "I'm not pulling over on the side of the road for him. Not safe. Not with how fast those cars go. Come on with you," she called into the buggy, putting out her arms.

First she lowered James to the ground, then Josiah, then lastly John-John. Joshua hadn't realized John-John had gone visiting with them. He was beginning to really take to the family and he fit in so well. He was so sweet to James and Josiah, protective of them and always kind. To have Joshua lose this family now would be such a blow to him.

"Josh," John-John called, though it came out sounding something like *Shosh*.

"John-John," Joshua said, emotion welling up in his throat. He swallowed hard.

Rosemary looked at Joshua and then at Phoebe's son. "Take the boys inside, John. That's it. Follow Jesse." She pointed toward the back door. "Josiah's just getting over his cold. I don't want him out here with it being so raw."

"Bye!" John-John called to Joshua, throwing up one hand covered with a blue mitten.

"See you later," Joshua responded in turn in English. John-John's English was coming along so well. He was so smart and such a fast learner.

Rosemary and Joshua both watched the boys toddle off, headed for the back door. Instead of following them, though, Rosemary came around to Joshua.

"You asked me how our visit at Lovey's was. It was nice." Beneath her chin, she tightened the black wool scarf she wore. "That Marshall, he's a good man. A good husband. Made a cradle for the babe who will be here in no time. Nice as I've ever seen. Properly Plain, of course, but still beautiful."

Joshua nodded and stroked Toby's nose, feeling a bit uncomfortable. He didn't know if Rosemary had heard the catch in his voice when he'd spoken to John-John, but why else would she be standing here looking at him the way she was. Ordinarily, she would have gone in with the boys.

Joshua cleared his throat, avoiding eye contact with his stepmother. "I should… I'll get Toby put up and give him a scoop of grain. Then back to the shop. Cold out here. I can't tell if it's going to snow or rain. Both maybe."

Rosemary was looking right at him. She nodded, but she made no move toward the house. She just stood there.

"Well…" he finally said, tightening his fingers around the horse's halter.

"*Ne*, not so fast, Joshua." Rosemary laid her hand on Toby's neck and gave him a pat. "Ordinarily, I'd let you hem and haw another few minutes, but it's too cold out here to wait on a Miller man. So out with it. I've things to get done in the house."

Joshua looked at her, startled. "Out with what?"

"How long have I known you, Joshua? Since you came into this world. I still remember walking into your mother's kitchen to see her wearing you on her front, with Jacob on her back, tied up with cloth. Wearing you the way English women wear their babies. You were always a sensitive one, even then." She looked up at him with her green eyes that seemed sometimes to be all-knowing. "Tell me what's wrong. Maybe I can help."

He lowered his head. "I…I'm fine."

She sighed. "Ah, a disagreement with Phoebe? I see it, you know. We all do. You like her. Truth be told, I think she's as sweet on you as you are on her."

To Joshua's embarrassment, his eyes suddenly got watery. He wiped at them with his sleeve. If he lost Phoebe, he didn't know what he would do. He'd be lost. Lost forever, maybe.

"Not Phoebe," he heard himself say. "Yes, Phoebe, but… Dat. Dat's the problem," he finally managed.

"Your father?" She sounded surprised. "You've had a disagreement with him? About what?"

For a moment, he hesitated. He liked Rosemary, *ne*, he loved her. He loved her because she loved his father, and because she treated Joshua and his brothers as if they were her own. He loved her because he knew, even though she'd never said so, that she loved him. But he had never talked to her about anything personal like this. Not about something so close to his heart. And he was so emotional right now that he didn't know that he wanted to. What if he actually cried? He'd never be able to face her again.

"Come out with it," she said quietly. "You'll feel better once you do. And you know I'll hear about it soon enough from your father. We don't keep things from each other."

He slowly lifted his gaze until it met hers, then he told her the whole story standing right there in the barnyard. And when he was done, she pointed at him sternly.

"Men," she muttered. "All right, let's go." She hooked her thumb in the direction of the lane.

"Go where?"

"To your father, of course. I'll not have this at my table nor in my house. So put up Toby and let's go see him now." She smiled kindly. "Together, *sohn*."

Not ten minutes later, Joshua stood at his father's closed workshop door again, this time with Rosemary at his side.

She rapped impatiently on the door with her knuckles. "Benjamin!"

"Rosemary?" he called from the other side of the door.

Joshua heard the sounds of a flurry of activity behind the door. He was hiding the Christmas gift, no doubt.

"What are you doing with the door closed?" She glanced at Joshua and then back at the door. "May I come in, husband?"

"Of course, Rosebud."

"Joshua's with me," she added, a hint of annoyance in her voice. "We're here to speak with you."

His father's heavy footsteps were followed by the door swinging open. Benjamin pulled off his glasses. "You're home from Lovey's."

"I don't have time for casual talk, Benjamin. I've supper to get ready." She strode into the shop, which, to Joshua's knowledge, she had never entered since they'd bought the property. Like her sewing room was her domain, the workshop was his father's.

Benjamin backed up and Joshua was surprised to see that the look on his father's face was one of apprehension. It wasn't that he seemed afraid of his wife, only...uneasy.

Inside the workshop, standing between a buggy

wheel set in a vise and the chair waiting to be repaired, Rosemary took up residence. She raised her hands to her hips and planted her feet squarely. "Joshua told me about your discussion and I have to say, Benjamin, I'd never want to side against you, you being the head of the family and all. Fact is, you and I rarely disagree, but I have to say—" she looked at him sternly "—you're flat-out wrong on this matter."

"Rosemary." Joshua's father sounded hurt, and Joshua suddenly felt bad for telling Rosemary about the conversation.

"Ben, you know I love you. Which means I have to tell you when you're wrong, the same as you need to tell me when I'm wrong. And I know as the head of the household, you're meant to be our spiritual leader. And you do a fine job of it. You've got a good head for God's words, but on this one…" She shook her head as if he was one of the little boys who had done something naughty. "You're flat-out wrong. That girl confessed her sin and she was granted forgiveness. It's plain as day. 'He that covereth his sins shall not prosper: but whoso confesseth and forsaketh them shall have mercy,'" she quoted from the Bible.

"Rosemary—" Benjamin said.

"'Who is a God like unto thee, that pardoneth iniquity, and passeth by the transgression of the remnant of his heritage?'" Rosemary went on, quoting another verse. "'He retaineth not his anger forever, because he delighteth in mercy.'"

Joshua's eyes widened in amazement. He knew few men besides his father who could quote word for word from the Bible. He wasn't sure he knew any woman who could quote much more than a few lines of psalms. It just wasn't something that was necessary. They had their preachers and bishops to quote from the good book.

"Rosebud," Benjamin said, his voice faltering.

She waggled her finger at him. "And the best one I can think of, Benjamin Miller? *'Forgive and you shall be forgiven'*!"

Benjamin hung his head and Joshua felt terrible.

"Dat, I'm so sorry," he said. "I didn't mean to—"

"Ne," his father interrupted. "I'm the one to apologize." He exhaled heavily. "To you. And to you as well, Rosemary. I've disappointed you."

She walked over and hugged him. Joshua's father wrapped his arms around his wife's waist. Joshua stared at the floor, feeling immensely uncomfortable and, at the same time, pleased that his father and stepmother could express their feelings for each other like this. Just when Joshua was beginning to wonder if he should leave them alone, Rosemary let go of her husband and stepped back.

"I'm not disappointed in you. It's not always easy to practice what we believe, Ben," Rosemary said, looking up at him. "I struggle every day. We all do."

"But this." Benjamin shook his head. "You know everything, I suppose?" he asked her.

She nodded. "Joshua told me you forbid him to marry Phoebe because of her past."

"It was my pride that set me on that path of thinking," Joshua's father said, speaking to him and Rosemary. "I...I was worried about what others might say. About my son. About our family."

"Anyone who's right with God, who knows God's word, would say good for you, Benjamin Miller." Rosemary drew her finger back and forth, pointing at him.

Joshua's father reached out and took his wife's hand. Then he turned to Joshua. "You were right, and I was wrong, son. We can't just say the words. We have to live them. God's word *does* tell us that we are forgiven for our sins. It was His son who made that possible." He shook his head slowly. "I don't know why God finds it so easy to forgive us and we find it so hard to forgive others."

"And sometimes ourselves," Rosemary put in gently.

"It's easy to quote God's word," Benjamin mused. "But not always easy to practice it."

Rosemary squeezed her husband's hand. "It's what makes us human."

"*Ya*, I suppose you're right." Joshua's father looked at Rosemary and then at Joshua again. "I was going to come to you, *sohn*. The minute you walked out of here, I realized how wrong I was. You should marry the woman you love. She's a good girl, your Phoebe. And she'll make a good wife to you. Her past is her past, and no matter how that little boy got here, he's still a gift from God. I truly believe that. I'm so sorry I've caused you pain. You have my blessing to wed Phoebe. I want you to marry the woman you love." Releasing his wife's hand, he took a step toward Joshua. "I'm sorry for this quarrel. I'm sorry for not being a better father to you, a better man." He glanced at Rosemary. "A better husband to you. And I hope that not only you two can forgive me, but Phoebe, too."

"*Atch*," Rosemary said, giving a wave of her hand.

"No need for Phoebe to even know about this. A little disagreement between father and son. It happens in a household full of men sometimes."

Joshua drew his hand across his eyes, overwhelmed with relief. His father had given him his approval to marry the woman he loved. Now all he had to do was tell Phoebe. "She already knows. I went right to her."

"Then go find her." Rosemary shooed him with a flutter of her hand. "And we'll talk about a wedding tonight at supper."

Just then, Bay walked into the shop. "Dat, Andy Byler wants to know if—" She halted and looked from one of them to the next and made a face. "What's going on? What are the three of you doing in here?"

"Mind your knitting," Rosemary warned.

"I'm going to find Phoebe," Joshua said, making for the door. "She's probably working on supper."

"Nope," Bay called after him.

Joshua turned back to his sister. "Then where is she?"

Bay pressed her lips together. She seemed to realize something serious was going on and her answer wasn't going to be one he wanted to hear. "Taken a buggy and gone."

"Gone *where*?" Joshua asked.

"Eli's," Bay said softly.

"No!" Joshua closed his eyes.

"What?" Benjamin asked. "What's the problem?"

"Eli," Joshua said, his stomach suddenly in his throat. He opened his eyes. "She's gone to accept Eli's marriage proposal."

"I thought she wanted to marry you," Rosemary said.

"She did. Does," Joshua managed. "But when I told

her that Dat was against it, she said she wouldn't come between us and…I guess she decided to accept Eli's offer." His hands fell to his sides. "I've lost her," he whispered.

"Stuff and nonsense!" Rosemary declared. "You haven't lost the girl until she stands before the bishop on her wedding day. Go, son. Go get her."

Joshua turned and strode through the door.

"Wait, *sohn*!" Benjamin declared. "I caused this mess. I'll go with you."

Rosemary watched her husband and son go out the shop door and then threw up her hands. "Looks like I may as well go, too!"

Chapter Twelve

Phoebe turned off the road into the driveway. Eli lived just off Route 8, a couple of roads over from the Miller harness shop. Phoebe had never been there, but they'd driven by his place. It was a small farm, maybe twenty-five acres with a neat little two-story square bunga-low and a series of typical Amish outbuildings: a dairy barn, a lean-to shed for farm equipment, a windmill, a chicken house and a woodshed. Everything was painted, neat and orderly, but what was interesting was that un-like most Amish houses that were painted white, his was a spruce green. There was a place to tie up in front of the enclosed porch.

A woolly black-and-white mixed-breed dog followed her buggy up the lane, and as she climbed out of the buggy, it greeted her with a wagging tail as it tried to nuzzle her hand. "Hello there," she said to the dog, giv-ing him a pet.

When she spoke, her voice sounded strange in her ears. She was nervous and scared. She was thinking that maybe this had been a bit impulsive, to come right to Eli. But the door she had thought had opened to a life with Joshua had closed, and she was determined not to let that destroy her the way John's death had nearly destroyed her. She was determined not to let her emotions get the best of her. She would not come between Joshua and his father. She wouldn't do it. So she wouldn't marry him and that was that. The good news was, she did not have to go back to Edom's home.

Eli wanted to marry her. He'd been straightforward about that. And, truthfully, a man like Eli was who she'd had in mind when she'd come to Hickory Grove in search of a husband. He was a man older than her, with children. He would make a good father to John-John and a good husband to her. And while there would probably never be the love between them that she had felt for John or Joshua, maybe she would come to love him in a different way. Women married for different reasons, especially Amish women. Not everyone found true love in the Englisher sense of the word, but a woman who married a good man, who had children with him, who had a good life trying to live God's words, could never ask for more.

"What's your name?" she asked the dog. "Are you a good boy?" She leaned one way and the other, trying to figure out if it was a boy or a girl. "Or are you a good girl?" she asked. Not able to tell, she walked up to the hitching post.

"A good girl," she heard a male voice say.

Phoebe looked up to see Eli standing on the porch steps, his hands in his pants pockets. He was wearing denim trousers and a faded green shirt that made his eyes seem bluer. His red beard was neatly trimmed, as was his hair. He smiled at her. "Her name is Molly. Found her in the parking lot at Byler's as a pup. Someone had dumped her." He came down the steps and walked over to take the leather strap from Phoebe and tie up her horse. "She was skinny and covered in fleas. But Lizzy wanted her." He shrugged. "So we took home from Byler's that day three pounds of lunch meat, a gallon of orange juice, a bag of peppermints and a puppy." He ticked the list off as he counted on his fingers.

Despite her nervousness, Phoebe couldn't help but smile. Eli was the kind of man who could put you at ease in a moment's time. She'd seen that the first night she had met him at the harvest supper at the Fishers'. "She seems like a nice dog. She followed me all the way in. She barked, but she wasn't mean about it."

"Just letting me know you had arrived." He smiled again. With the horse tied up, he turned to her. "I was waiting for you."

"You were?" She pulled her black wool cloak tighter and looked up at him. She'd not bothered to fetch her good hat. She really wasn't dressed properly to be visiting a man. She was just wearing her blue scarf tied at the nape of her neck and a heavy black wool one tied under her chin. She'd left the Miller house in haste, half afraid she would back out if she let herself think on the matter too long. By the time she had reached his driveway, she'd been worried she had made a mistake in coming. But now that he was standing here, she thought maybe she wasn't; maybe he could help her forget about her love for Joshua. Of course, she could never forget it or forget him, but maybe the pain she felt right now could be eased with time the way the pain of her loss of John had eased over time.

"Well," Eli said, glancing out into the pretty little barnyard. "I guess what I mean is, I was *hoping* you would come. I was hoping you would change your mind about marrying me."

She'd had this plan to come here and tell him she would marry him, but she'd not thought about how she would say it. He was making it easy for her, bless him. "How do you know that's why I'm here?" she heard herself say. She wasn't sure why she was delaying. "I might have been coming to bring you some of Rosemary's cranberry-nut bread. She drizzles an orange icing over the top."

He studied her with his blue eyes that were a different shade than her own. He had nice eyelashes. She could see that standing so close to him. And freckles.

"*Did* you bring me some of Rosemary's cranberry bread?" he asked.

She shook her head.

"Then why—"

Molly suddenly shot into the driveway, barking, and headed down the lane.

Phoebe turned to look to see what she had gone after and heard the familiar sound of hoofbeats and the creak of a buggy. Someone was coming up Eli's lane and fast. "Who would be—"

"It's Benjamin's buggy," Eli said.

Phoebe couldn't help but hear a sound of disappointment in his voice. Of sadness. "Benjamin is here?" she asked, confused. Benjamin never drove like that. He always drove slowly and cautiously, as if he had all the time in the world.

"Not Benjamin," Eli said with a sigh. "Your Joshua, I suspect."

Phoebe didn't know what to say. She didn't really need to say anything. The buggy came to an abrupt stop in the middle of the barnyard, and the driver's door slid open and Benjamin heaved himself to the ground. He was wearing the same kind of knit hat Joshua and all of his brothers wore, but Benjamin couldn't be mistaken for anyone else with his stocky frame and rusty-colored graying beard.

"Benjamin," Eli said, seeming as surprised to see him as Phoebe was.

Molly bounded around the buggy, continuing to bark. Benjamin's gelding, Toby, danced in his traces but remained in place.

As Benjamin hurried toward them, the passenger-side door slid open and Rosemary leaped out.

"Rosemary?" Phoebe said. What was going on? Had Rosemary and Benjamin figured out what she was doing and come to warn Eli that he shouldn't take her as his wife?

Instead of following Rosemary and Benjamin, Molly moved to the rear of the buggy and began to bark even louder.

Two little boys who looked like miniature versions of Eli appeared on the porch steps. Both were wearing knitted slippers. Neither was wearing a coat.

"Who has come?" asked the taller of the two boys in Pennsylvania *Deutsch*. He looked to be six or seven and had hair the same color as Eli's. The smaller boy's was more of a strawberry blonde.

"You shouldn't be outside without coats," Eli told his sons above the din of Molly's barking. He clapped his hands. "Molly, come, girl!"

But the dog didn't budge. She just kept barking at the back of the buggy. Then the door swung open and Phoebe's heart felt as if it skipped a beat. It was Joshua. Her Joshua!

"Neighbor," Benjamin said, striding toward them. "I am sorry to kick up such a fuss in your yard, but I've... We need to speak to—"

"Phoebe," Eli finished for him. He smiled what seemed like a sad smile to her and glanced her way. "I wish you nothing but happiness, Phoebe," he said.

"But..." Phoebe didn't know what say. She didn't know what was going on.

"Life's funny sometimes, isn't it?" Eli said softly to her. There was a twinkle in his blue eyes now. "You think life is going to go one way and then it takes a turn like a bend in a river, and all of sudden you're floating in that direction. It's not a bad place to be, just different than you thought. Sometimes different than you thought you wanted." He turned toward the house just as Joshua reached her side. "I'll leave you all to your family business," he said. Then he opened his arms and herded his boys toward the door. "Who wants hot chocolate with big, fat marshmallows?"

"Me! Me!" the little boys cried, bouncing up and down as they followed their father into the house.

"Phoebe," Joshua said.

She turned to him, pressing her lips together. She

wanted so badly to think Benjamin had had a change of heart, but what if that wasn't why he was here?

"My *vadder* has given us his blessing. To marry," Joshua said in a rush as he reached for her hands. "Please tell me you didn't tell Eli you would marry him."

"I want to apologize to you, Phoebe," Benjamin interrupted, walking up to them.

Rosemary moved to her husband's side.

"I want to apologize for my failings. I like to say I know God's word. I try to follow it each and every day, but the truth is, I fall short sometimes. A lot of times," he said.

To Phoebe's surprise, she could see that the older man's eyes were tearing up. And as with Joshua when he had done the same down in the cellar earlier in the day, she found herself liking Benjamin even more. Maybe loving him in a way that she had never loved a man before, the way a woman loved her father. "It's all right," she whispered.

"*Ne*, it's not," he told her firmly. "As the head of my household, I'm supposed to be the one to set a good example. I've been preaching to my boys since they were babes the merits of forgiveness. It's easy to forgive someone for spilled milk or a misplaced word, but the true test comes at times like this. And—" The older man looked away for a moment, seeming to be overcome by emotion. But when he looked at her again, he didn't seem weak the way Phoebe thought emotion could make a person—he seemed stronger. Stronger than before. "All I can do is say I'm sorry and hope you can forgive me. Hope that with the Lord's help, I can be a better man tomorrow."

Phoebe nodded to Benjamin. "Of course I forgive you."

"Then you'll do me the honor of being my daughter-in-law?"

"Benjamin!" Rosemary cried. "You're not supposed to ask her that." She gave Joshua a little push. "That's for him to ask." She looped her arms through her husband's. "Now let's go inside and make a proper apology to Eli and leave these two alone. I imagine Eli has an extra hot chocolate or two."

Benjamin looked to his son. "I want to say thank you," he said.

"For what?" Joshua asked.

"For being my son. For being the man you are. You know, a father's greatest wish is that his sons will be better men than he is."

Joshua started to say something, but Phoebe caught his eye and he stayed silent. Then he slipped her hand into his and they watched Rosemary and Benjamin, hand in hand, go up the steps and into the house. Then he turned to her. "So…" he said.

"So," Phoebe echoed. Something brushed her leg, and she looked down to see the black-and-white dog plop herself down and lean against her. She looked up into Joshua's eyes again.

He wrapped his arms around her waist. "I'll ask again. Did you tell Eli you would marry him?"

She shook her head, thinking how good his touch felt.

"Did you come here to do that?" Joshua pressed.

She nodded.

"Would you have told him, had we not arrived when we did?"

"I don't know," she answered honestly.

Joshua gazed into her eyes, his brown eyes warm with caring. With love for her. "I guess I'd better make haste then." He drew the back of his hand against her cheek. "Will you marry me, Phoebe Miller?"

"I will, Joshua Miller."

The corner of his mouth turned up in a smile. "Well, this will be convenient."

She smiled at him, not sure what he meant. "What?"

"You won't have to change your name. When we wed."

She laughed. "I hadn't thought about that. It *is* convenient."

"It is," he said as he wrapped his arms around her and drew her tightly against him. "Don't suppose I can have that kiss now?" he whispered in her ear.

"Not until we're married," she whispered back.

He laughed softly, and as Phoebe slid her arms around Joshua's neck and hugged him tightly, she realized that God had more than answered her prayers because she had not only found a father for her son, but a man to love.

Epilogue

Miller's Greenhouse
One year later

Joshua carried a huge white poinsettia in an eight-inch pot in each arm. "Here you go," he said, walking up to the front counter where Phoebe had been stationed all day. With only four days before Christmas, they had been busy since early morning. Thanks to Bay's idea of giving away a few poinsettias to stores around Dover, she'd generated more business than they could handle. Everyone was coming to Miller's Greenhouse to buy the healthy, beautiful poinsettias Joshua Miller was growing.

"This is the last of the big white ones," he told Phoebe as he set them on the counter. "We'll have to be sure to grow more next year." He pulled off his knit cap and scratched his head. "I never thought they would sell so well."

"The customer will be right back in to get them," she said, using a red pen to add to the tally they were keeping on a notepad beside the register. Joshua wanted to know how many of each color and in which sizes they sold so they would be better prepared the following Christmas season. It had been Phoebe's idea to keep a paper tally because the cash register only recorded the size of the plants they sold, not the color.

"One," John-John said, pushing a tiny white poinsettia onto the counter. "For Mam."

"Goodness, I didn't even see you there," she said, peering over the counter at her son. "Joshua, I thought you sent him up to the house."

Her husband shrugged and lifted the boy into his arms. "He wanted to help me move the last of the poinsettias to this end of the greenhouse."

Phoebe brought the edges of the sweatshirt of Joshua's that she was wearing closer across her rounded belly. Two weeks ago, it had still zipped up, but there was no zipping it now. Something she knew Eunice Gruber would comment on at church the next Sunday. There had been talk that it was inappropriate for Phoebe to be working in the greenhouse now that it was obvious to everyone that she was in the family way. Joshua had disagreed and that had been the end of the matter. He said he loved spending his days with his wife beside him, and it wasn't up to Eunice or anyone else in Hickory Grove as to where his wife worked.

"You think we'll run out of poinsettias?" Phoebe asked.

"Ne," Joshua told her. "But I think we'll sell the very last ones tomorrow before we close shop."

They had all worked so hard that fall to grow the Christmas flowers—and make the wreaths and garlands—that they had agreed they would close on December 23 and not open again until April 1 when seedlings would be available. If the weather held out, that would give them a chance to get another greenhouse put up in time for the spring plantings.

"Phoebe, do we have any more red gingham bows?" Bay asked as she walked into their shop off the side of the greenhouse, which wasn't much more than a shed. She was carrying in each arm several wreaths made from local pine trees. "I thought I had two more."

Phoebe leaned around Joshua to address her sister-in-law. "Last customer bought them."

Bay dropped the unadorned wreaths onto a small worktable they used for customizing the greenery. "We're selling bows now?"

Phoebe grimaced, afraid she'd overstepped her bounds. "She paid five dollars apiece for them."

Bay's face lit up. "Well, in that case, we're selling pre-tied bows now." She looked at her brother. "Good thing you married her, Joshua. She's got a head for business."

Joshua turned to look at Phoebe and grinned. "*Ya*, good thing I married her."

Bay sighed. "I guess I'll run up to the house and see if Mam has any more ribbon I can use. I hate to have to run into Dover to buy more."

"You mind taking this pup up to the house with you?" Joshua asked, bouncing John-John on his hip.

"This pup?" Bay asked, walking over to give him a tickle on his tummy.

John giggled.

"This one?" she said, giving him another poke.

Joshua lowered John to the ground, pulled a small knit cap from his pocket and tugged it down over the little boy's head. "Go with Bay up to the house. And do not wear those boots into Rosemary's kitchen again," he warned. "Else you'll be sleeping outside tonight with Silas and Adah."

John knitted his brows. "But I want to stay here and help," he said in near-perfect English.

"Listen to your *dat*," Phoebe warned.

"*Ya*, Dat," John said obediently. Then he slipped his hand into Bay's.

"Be back in a few minutes," Bay told them.

Phoebe watched them walk out the door, the bell overhead jingling as it opened and closed. When she and Joshua were alone, she leaned over, pressing her elbows to the counter. "I'm proud of you," she said softly.

"Of me?" He leaned over from the opposite side.

"Of you," she said, smiling, gazing into his beautiful brown eyes.

"And why is that?" he asked.

She shrugged. "Let's see…because this greenhouse has turned out to be a bigger success than any of us expected. *Including* you and Bay."

"Uh-huh. What else?"

"And because you've taken so well to being a father."

"Good thing," he teased, looking down at her belly.

She giggled. "And because you're the finest husband a woman could ask for."

"Am I now?" He walked around the counter and opened his arms to her.

"We're in the shop," she whispered. "Have you no

shame?" But as she spoke the words, she stepped into his arms.

"Just a quick kiss, that's all I need." He held her tightly, looking into her eyes. "It's okay for me to kiss you, right?" he teased. "Because we're married now?"

Phoebe answered him with a soft kiss on his mouth and the unspoken promise that their love would only grow with the years.

* * * * *

*If you loved this book,
pick up Emma Miller's previous book*
The Amish Spinster's Courtship

*And check out these other stories of Amish life
from The Amish Matchmaker miniseries*

A Match for Addy
A Husband for Mari
A Beau for Katie
A Love for Leah
A Groom for Ruby

Available now from Love Inspired!

Find more great reads at www.Harlequin.com

Dear Reader,

I hope Joshua and Phoebe's story touched your heart the way it touched mine. Their story reminds me that, as humans, we all make mistakes and that we all can be forgiven and must forgive. In this world we live in today, this is a message of hope for me.

My next visit to the Miller family involves Benjamin's eldest son, Ethan, who is Hickory Grove's schoolmaster. Ethan lost his wife years ago and hasn't been able to find his way out of that darkness. His family is encouraging him to marry again, but no one has come along to tug at his heartstrings. Then a naughty little boy joins his classroom and, at his wits end, Ethan joins forces with Jamie's widowed mother, Abigail, to improve the child's behavior. While Abigail and Ethan are at odds at first, they quickly become friends, then fall in love. But love is complicated, and Abigail and Ethan have to make their way through several obstacles to find happiness again.

I'm excited about Abigail and Ethan's journey. I hope you'll join me again in Hickory Grove to find out if love really can conquer all.

Peace be with you,

Emma Miller

Get 4 FREE REWARDS!

We'll send you 2 FREE Books plus 2 FREE Mystery Gifts.

Love Inspired® books feature contemporary inspirational romances with Christian characters facing the challenges of life and love.

FREE
Value Over
$20

*Carolyn Wiebe will do anything to protect her late
sister's children from their abusive father—even give
up her Amish roots and pretend to be Mennonite.
But when she starts falling for Amish bachelor
Michael Miller, can they conquer their pasts—and her
secrets—by Christmas to build a forever family?*

Read on for a sneak preview of
An Amish Christmas Promise *by Jo Ann Brown,
available December 2019 from Love Inspired!*

"Are the *kinder* okay?"

"Yes, they'll be fine." Uncomfortable with his small
intrusion into her family, she said, "Kevin had a bad
dream and woke us up."

"Because of the rain?"

She wanted to say that was silly but, glad she could be
honest with Michael, she said, "It's possible."

"Rebuilding a structure is easy. Rebuilding one's sense
of security isn't."

"That sounds like the voice of experience."

"My parents died when I was young, and both my
twin brother and I had to learn not to expect something
horrible was going to happen without warning."

"I'm sorry. I should have asked more about you and
the other volunteers. I've been wrapped up in my own
tragedy."

"At times like this, nobody expects you to be thinking of anything but getting a roof over your *kinder*'s heads."

He didn't reach out to touch her, but she was aware of every inch of him so close to her. His quiet strength had awed her from the beginning. As she'd come to know him better, his fundamental decency had impressed her more. He was a man she believed she could trust.

She shoved that thought aside. Trusting any man would be the worst thing she could do after seeing what Mamm had endured during her marriage and then struggling to help her sister escape her abusive husband.

"I'm glad you understand why I must focus on rebuilding a life for the children." The simple statement left no room for misinterpretation. "The flood will always be a part of us, but I want to help them learn how to live with their memories."

"I can't imagine what it was like."

"I can't forget what it was like."

Normally she would have been bothered by someone having sympathy for her, but if pitying her kept Michael from looking at her with his brown puppy-dog eyes that urged her to trust him, she'd accept it. She couldn't trust any man, because she wouldn't let the children spend their lives witnessing what she had.

Don't miss
An Amish Christmas Promise *by Jo Ann Brown,*
available December 2019 wherever
Love Inspired® *books and ebooks are sold.*

LoveInspired.com

LIEXP1119

SPECIAL EXCERPT FROM

Love Inspired
SUSPENSE

*When a police detective stumbles upon a murder scene
with no body, can the secret father of her child help her
solve the case without becoming the next victim?*

Read on for a sneak preview of
Holiday Homecoming Secrets *by Lynette Eason,*
available December 2019 from Love Inspired Suspense.

Bryce Kingsley bolted toward the opening of the deserted
mill and stepped inside, keeping one hand on the weapon
at his side. "Jade?"

"Back here." Her voice reached him, sounding weak,
shaky.

He hurried to her, keeping an eye on the surrounding
area. Bryce rounded the end of the spindle row to see
Jade on the floor, holding her head. Blood smeared a short
path down her cheek. "You're hurt!" For a moment, she
simply stared up at him, complete shock written across
her features. "Jade? Hello?"

She blinked. "Bryce?"

"Hi." He glanced over his shoulder, then swung the
beam of the flashlight over the rest of the interior.

"You're here?"

"Yeah. This wasn't exactly the way I wanted to let you
know I was coming home, but—"

"What are you doing here?"

"Can we discuss that later? Let's focus on you and the
fact you're bleeding from a head wound."

"I…I'm all right."

"Did you get a look at who hit you?"

"No."

A car door slammed. Blue lights whirled through the broken windows and bounced off the concrete-and-brick walls. Bryce helped her to her feet. "Let's get that head looked at."

"Wait." He could see her pulling herself together, the shock of his appearance fading. "I need to take a look at something."

He frowned. "Okay." She went to the old trunk next to the wall. "What is it?"

"The person who hit me was very interested in whatever was over here."

Bryce nodded to the shovel and disturbed dirt in front of the trunk. "Looks like he was trying to dig something up."

"What does this look like to you?"

"Looks like someone's been digging."

"Yes, but why? What could they possibly be looking for out here?"

"Who knows?" Bryce studied the pile of dirt and the bricks. "Actually, I don't think they were looking for anything. I think they were in the middle of *burying* something."

Don't miss
Holiday Homecoming Secrets *by Lynette Eason,*
available December 2019 wherever
Love Inspired® Suspense books and ebooks are sold.

LoveInspired.com